AF373879

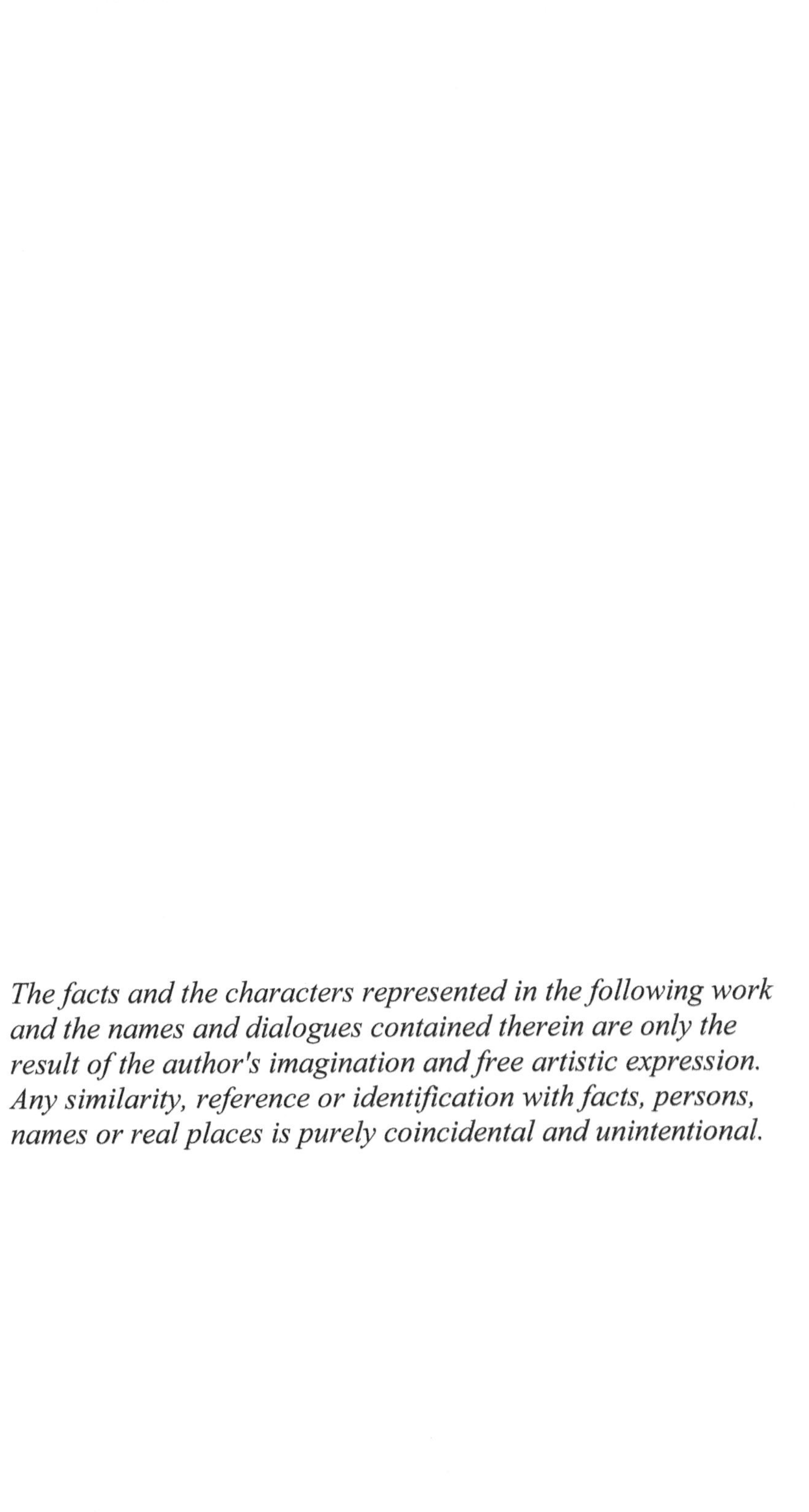

The facts and the characters represented in the following work and the names and dialogues contained therein are only the result of the author's imagination and free artistic expression. Any similarity, reference or identification with facts, persons, names or real places is purely coincidental and unintentional.

To the Memory

FOREWORD

It will not be necessary for readers to reread this story because its characters, the Santonocito, thanks to the masterful pen of the writer, will remain forever carved in the memory, but especially in the heart of each one of us.

Their story takes off from a town near Fucecchio: the "Pinete" (Pinewoods). From here, they will leave for Tunis, as emigrants, one after the other, two sisters: Giulia and Maria Bandini.

*The story of **Giulia,** an authentic heroine of this unforgettable story, will touch us in the most intimate layers. I also cried when Giulia and Prof. Calò met again a few days before the professor's death, in Tunis. I cried because in Giulia's life there was never a place for dreams and an existence without "dreams" becomes a daily inferno.*

***Maria** Bandini, married in Tunis soon after the end of the First World War with Salvatore Santonocito, who emigrated to Tunis from Palermo, will become one of the two pillars of the Santonocito family. Maria is the living Archangel of devotion: devotion to her husband and to his beliefs; absolute devotion to the family; devotion, above all, to God. According to Maria, nothing was entrusted to fate: in all, even in the most tragic events, she knew how to read and see God's loving hand.*

***Salvatore**, the bricklayer, is the other pillar. Undisputed hero of the First World War became a helpless victim of the Second World War as equally. Only the intercession of his son Angelo will spare him the tremendous experience of the concentration camp near Tunis. The divinities of his religion were the family, the homeland Sicily, and work. The poignant passion for*

Maria, the Tuscan emigrant he had fallen in love with, made him overcome illiteracy. He wanted to learn how to write in order to communicate with his beloved Maria. The fire of Love made him even unconquered, invulnerable. Salvatore cultivated also in his children his other great passion, after that of work and the Sea. None of the four sons nor Pina, the daughter, remained free from this passion. The writer had the great merit of having seized his character in very few but significant acts of his existence.

Angelo, the firstborn of the Santonocito family will become the exemplary angel that protect the family and the community. Wonderful the portrait that gives us the writer. Unforgettable will also remain the poem dedicated to him by his brother Umberto and the weeping of his dog who wanted to irrevocably share the fate of death with him.

Candido, the second son, stubborn, obstinate, wanted to be a paratrooper of the "Folgore" a protagonist of World War II. He will end, after the war, in a section of the asylum of S. Salvi in Florence. The writer will make us touch with hand the ravine that lurked there before the closure of all the insane asylums that took place in 1978 in Italy. "Horresco Referens" would have written the Latin poet Virgil.

Pina: the sea, the deception, an overwhelming love realized only in half, the dedication to the family and then to the brother that will become priest, Ferdinando. In this, all her existence is synthesized. A heroine? maybe. But tacit. None of those who had the opportunity to know her would have ever imagined that under the ashes of her appearance there was or had been a volcanic fire. I will always bring with me the image of Pina that with amazement arrange in a box her two twin brothers born dead. Perhaps on that occasion in the heart of

Pina also died the sea, the deception and the overwhelming love that had given meaning and taste to her existence.

Ferdinando*. is the mother's spiritual heir. The writer of this throbbing story, shows him a boy, intent on interpreting the role of a priest. The sea and the celebration of the Catholic rites were the two great passions of that boy born in Tunis on June 18, 1932. He will become a priest years later and now a famous poet.*

Umberto*. is the father of the writer. In the very few pages dedicated to her father, the writer turned out to be a candidate as a film novelist. The form adopted will result incredibly significant. The description of the College of Cortona run by nuns where Umberto was accompanied by his mother Maria, is chilling. Umberto managed to send his mother a note where he wrote, "Mother, I can't live without you. Either you come and take me home or I will escape." Maria went and took him away.*

Even in the stories of seemingly common persons "shine" in a manner sometimes sparkling feelings of unsuspected dimension and value, lived rather than confirmed, this is the great message of the writer.

Mario Catastini

Fucecchio, June 20th, 2012

Chapter 1 : The Bandini Sisters

Cherubina Niccoletti (called Carruba) was born in 1863 in Pinewood, a small village in the heart of the forest of Cerbaie a few kilometers from the swamp of Fucecchio. The Cerbaie comprised two-thirds of the municipal territory of Fucecchio: low hills with a sweet profile, which stretched between the basin of the former swamp of Bientina and that of Fucecchio. It was an area largely covered by a high-stem forest of (maritime pines, quercus, oak) trees. From Pinewood to Galleno you could pass through a narrow path a short cut skirted by very high pine trees where you could find all sort of wagons pulled by cows, to barouche loaded with chopped wood that came and went from the various destinations, to kids playing merrily hide and seek.

Carruba was an austere woman: no one remembered having ever seen her smile. She had brown hair always collected at the nape and the long furrows of wrinkles on the side of the mouth expressed so much sadness and little inclination for dialogue. She had married Candido Bandini, also from Pinewood, fifteen years older. Candido, owner of several plots of land had been considered a gold bachelor, also appreciated by the young ladies of the neighbouring surroundings; but he had always considered marriage a waste of time, at least until he met Carruba.

He had pale skin and eyes of a celestial blue almost transparent like water: perhaps for this he had been called Candido (meaning Candide), and never name had been more appropriate. Hard worker, had seen the family grow very fast maybe due to the unexpressed desire for a male son which never arrived. Everyone, within the Bandini family, had a very precise role, daughters included as the age allowed. But one day a sudden illness took him to an early graveyard. Candido left Carruba and five daughters: the eldest was twenty years old.

At that time there was no room for despair or to fall into depression: it was necessary to move forward at all costs. The younger ones were hungry and their survival was a must for the widowed mother. Carruba relied heavily on Elettra, the eldest, who looked like a reincarnation of her father: she was patient, always had the right word for all, adored the sisters and had a strong sense of responsibility inherited from Candido. During the day she behaved in a flawless manner and showed herself attentive to the needs of others; but at night time she gave free rein to tears and despair. Maria, the sister who slept with her, felt all this, but respecting her outburst did not interfere, all she could do was to pray and call all the saints for their support, which she would continue to do for the rest of her life.

Elettra could not avoid remembering when at the end of the day her father would sit in his armchair in the kitchen and with his daughters sitting on the floor or next to the fireplace would begin to tell stories happened to members of the family even if never known; but the atmosphere created was beautiful with the soft light lit by the candles and the creaking of burning wood. The smaller sisters Nandina and Angiolina would invariably fall asleep to the warmth created and Giulia would start to fantasize, perhaps it was during those tales and in those evenings that she began to develop her fervent imagination and fancifulness.

Nandina was jovial and carefree; perhaps her twelve years just did not allow her to fully understand what was happening around her even if she strongly missed the father, her happy character did not allow her to get too gloomy: in her mind the father had gone far away but then surely one day would have returned. It was enough for her to go on and wait while thinking of everyday life. In the end she was not alone: she had her mother and all the sisters. She was muffled and insensitive to the outside world.

One evening something happened that made everyone understand that the father would have never returned. For those who had set aside the thought, for those who kept busy in order not to think about it, the incident brought all to a firm point from which to start again. The dinner was served as usual: a single dish, mainly soup, while for the younger children even some fruit and cheese. Each would then set up the kitchen while Carruba washed the dishes; but that evening they were all attracted by a noise that came from near chimney: they turned almost at the same time and saw Angiolina, of just five years old, standing up on the father's armchair, staring at all with her large celestial eyes and black curly hair. She was swinging on the armchair against the wall, just to draw the attention of those in the room. They realized at that moment that Angiolina for all the past months since the death of the father had never cried or asked anyone questions about what had happened. She had always been an introverted and silent child, observing the world as a spectator rather than living it. She would follow Nandina everywhere all day long always in strict silence.

Now she was standing on her father's armchair drawing attention to herself as she had never done before. A tear descended on her pink cheek and while everyone looked at her incredulously she said:

"Father, is dead"!

One Sunday at the exit of the Holy Mass, Giulia noticed a ticket hanging from the small wooden bulletin board that she had never noticed before. The small bulletin board was the newsletter of the small village and the surrounding County: there you could browse through marriage and death announcements,

just to have something to talk about in the evening.
The ticket said:

*"Italian-French families in Tunis,
looking for housekeepers and child care.
Monthly departures by Sea. For more information
please contact the local priest Don Ettore"*

Giulia immediately felt a strong attraction for that
name, Tunis. She didn't know where it was but she
had heard that it was somewhere in Africa. Giulia
informed Elettra and Maria about the message, but
they did not put a great emphasis on it: for them the
everyday life was of priMaria interest. Giulia then,
tried to involve Carruba: every opportunity was good
enough to mention the subject. In every speech she
tried to gain more information and wanted to talk
with Ettore the Don on the issue of Tunis. Also for
Carruba, Tunis sounded like a very far place, so
didn't give much importance to Giulia.

Some time went by and Giulia seemed to have set
aside the idea of taking an interest on Tunis when she
found herself in the confessional with Don Ettore.
Don Ettore was a very modern priest for that time. He
had fostered the care of other churches scattered
throughout the various surroundings and always ran
like crazy. Full of initiatives he had grouped the
various young men and girls to form a choral and

tried to bring them in the various initiatives. He was rather small and wide; with his brisk walk he was seen swinging with his long black outfit all the way down the street. Affectionately the villagers loved to say: "there goes pendulum".

At the end of the confession, Giulia found the courage to ask Don Ettore more information about the ticket hanging on the bulletin board and he gave her so many information that she could scarcely remember everything when in the evening at dinner Giulia tried to address the topic Tunis with her mother and sisters. Don Ettore had seen in Giulia a real interest for that opportunity, but knew the Bandini family well and knew in his heart that it would have been difficult for Giulia to convince his mother and sister Elettra, two authentic pillars of firmness. For this reason he had offered to speak, himself, to the family. Giulia with her independent spirit decided to try alone to face all and only after she would have accepted the help of Don Ettore.

It was really a difficult feat to convince the stubborn Carruba and the irreducible Elettra: Giulia softened the ground, the rest was done in the following days by Don Ettore.

No one, apart from Don Ettore, had noticed that Elettra was in love with a young man who sang in the choir; but Don Ettore had observed them for some time. The young man, the son of the sawmill owner who gave a lot of work to everyone in the village, was called Orpheus and for Elettra it would have been a very good arrangement, thought by Don Ettore. Unfortunately, the sense of responsibility shown by Elettra towards the family would have hindered the project of a marriage. On the other side also Giulia was grown up by now and at eighteen many of her friends were already married or at service.

In the weeks that followed, Don Ettore made work of persuasion on Carruba. He talked about the daughters, on how they had grown up, about some work they could do, the possibility of a marriage and finally brought down the speech on Tunis. Although struggling Carruba had realized that her daughters were growing up and that she could not keep them with her for much longer, but she also wanted to see them happy. For a long time a man had not entered into their family and the words of Don Ettore made a breach on her reticence.

Nevertheless Giulia was not the only one to have noticed that ticket in the bulletin board and soon all over the village everyone was only talking about this, going to service in those wealthy families in Tunis, where everything was paid for, even the trip expenses plus food and lodging, in addition to a monthly fee.

Starting from the Unification of Italy (1861) there had been a considerable emigration of Italian and French for Tunis, but especially the Genoese first and Sicilian after had made a real Colony over there, near the *"Goulette"* about ten kilometers from the periphery Northern of Tunis. Soon after the Italians would have reached the remarkable figure of about 100,000 in the early twentieth century

Giulia obtained permission to leave her family with the blessing of Don Ettore in 1912. With sadness in her heart but carefree due to the young age she began to prepare for that long-awaited departure.

During the Christmas festivities the choir had often gathered for the singing rehearsals and Elettra had accompanied Maria during the various preparations in the Church. It was really difficult to hide the feelings that were growing between Elettra and Orpheus. One evening Orpheus, left alone with Don Ettore, revealed his feelings to him:

"I want to marry Elettra", he began.

He then continued by decanting her beauty. He confessed the sentiment that for so many months was burning in his heart and being shy had prevented him from declaring his intentions to Elettra. Of course he could not hide his reluctance against Carruba which seemed to him a real Cerberus.

Don Ettore promised the boy that he would speak with Elettra and with Carruba about his intentions and so he did.

The marriage of Elettra and Orpheus took place with a great haste in January of the new year to allow Giulia to participate before her departure for Tunis at the beginning of spring. All expenses were supported by the bridegroom and Carruba was happy to see her daughter settled even though her heart was full with worries for her other daughter next to departure. Maria and the small Nandina and Angiolina would remain at her side and this gave her great comfort.

The morning of the wedding everything had been prepared with simplicity and precision. Elettra had a long white dress with a tight bodice and skirt that widened slightly. The bodice with the raised collar made her figure even more slender. The hair gathered behind the nape sprouted just below the long veil of lace. In her hands little white gloves.

Nandina and Angiolina had been dressed in a white muslin dress just below the knee and in their loose hair a little crown of flowers. Being January and quite cold, under the muslin dress they had a wool camisole that made them look even more chubby and padded than they actually were.

Orpheus waited impatiently at the entrance of the church: he would have walked with Elettra up the church aisle as tradition imposed. The ceremony of Don Ettore made young and old emotional and cry, he could really touch the hearts of everyone!

At the end of the evening, while everyone greeted each other and returned to their homes, Angiolina broke into a desperate weeping. The little girl had observed everything during the party, but she had not understood much of what was going on. Everyone smiled and complimented, kissed, but despite the festive appearance, she felt so much sadness inside but did not know why.

Only one other time she had felt so desperate, it had been when she had truly perceived the loss of her father; now although in a situation of joy, she was feeling that she was losing something again.

Spring came again. The ship for Tunis departed from the port of Livorno and made a stopover in Palermo in Sicily, where the majority of the immigrants embarked. The crossing would last almost two days.

On that morning the sky was grey and a light rain wet the fields already plowed. Carruba did not accompany her daughter, but preferred to greet her from home as well as the small girls: it would have been too painful to see the ship move away from the port. Only Maria and Elettra went with Giulia among the others of the village that were leaving with her. Don Ettore came to greet her but remained waiting outside the house. When she passed by, he hugged her for a long time and gave her a kiss on her forehead. He had seen these girls grow up and was very fond of him.

Giulia and her sisters had never been to the port of Livorno even if not so far away from home and never seen a ship before. Everything looked huge and they had never seen so many people all together. There was danger of getting lost in that crowd: so they held hands. Giulia's heart was beating fast for the emotion. She had long awaited this moment, wanted it, desired it, she felt that her life was at a turning point, and she was eager to meet her destiny, whatever it was.

The ship departed punctually. A pale sun overlooked the clouds and all the people on the bridge greeted those who had remained on the ground, waving handkerchiefs in the air between tears and smiles. For many of them that would have been a journey from which they would have never returned.

Chapter 2 : the Santonocito

They arrived in Tunis. Situated on the shores of a lagoon near the ancient Carthage, Tunis was united with the Mediterranean Sea by a navigable canal of about 10 km that connected it to the "*Goulette*". The surroundings of the city appeared rich in vineyards and olive groves. Once landed off the ship a warm breath full of salt invested their faces; they felt immediately that the climate was different from the known one. Despite the beginning of Spring the sun emanated a heat that in Italy was felt only in august.

The first thing that struck Giulia was the white of the houses and the absence of the roofs. She was accustomed to seeing sloping roofs covered with tiles: instead you could see rows of colored cloths spread out to dry. In the air a strong smell of tobacco and spices.

All around her a multitude of persons mostly with dark skin, natives and those recently arrived already with a sunburnt skin. Half naked barefoot children ran from all sides and the beasts with their sickening odor were amalgamated along with the crowd.

Giulia was holding a leaflet given to her by Don Ettore with all the indications on how to reach the house of the family to which she would serve.

When she started talking to a stranger, she was surprised to hear him speak Italian. She soon realized that almost everyone spoke Italian or understood it. The mass of emigration had developed mainly from Sicily after 1878 when thousands of workers had moved for the construction of the railway which from Tunis was directed towards the Algerian border. This was the most extensive migratory movement of workers that occurred immediately after the imposition of the Protectorate.

The family to which Giulia had been assigned was that of an Italian doctor married to a French woman. Their surnames were Calò-Cordier and they had two young children. Giulia would take care of them and help in the kitchen since the Italian food was the favorite. The two kids went to a French school. Giulia had to accompany them and pick them up at the end of the lessons plus speak to them only in Italian language, the mother-tongue of their father.

The house, a pleasant 3 floor building with a small garden and some palm trees, was in the *"Bardo"* area near the famous archeological museum. On the top floor lived the doctor's father, widower, also a doctor himself, now retired.

Giulia was immediately very well accepted. Everyone was friendly to her and the kids loved her cooking. The only one who looked at her without ever a smile, but scrutinized her attentively, was the old Doctor Calò.

Giulia immediately began to write long descriptive letters to the family of the place and the persons she found but at the same time reassuring everyone thinking about how Carruba could be worried for her.

One day the family took Giulia to the "*Medina*" and she remained literally fascinated.
Walking through the street she saw the wonderful and mysterious colored doors. Those doors communicated something mysterious, something impenetrable, referring to hundred of meanings according to the local beliefs, especially of what they hid behind. Simple doors, colored, yellow, green, rectangular, double doors, all with a small door beneath.

The latter door, they told her, had been the result of the cunning of a woman, which had remained for centuries in the culture of the Tunisian doors. The legend said that the little door made in the main side of the door was invented by the intelligence of a Spanish princess, a bride to the "*Bey*" of Tunis. She had been indignant at the attitude of her Muslim subjects, who never bowed before anyone, not even in the presence of the sovereign. Then contrived this little door that being smaller than normal, would have forced everyone to bend and bow.

After that visit to the "*Medina*", Giulia spent many sleepless nights. Her fantasy flew and, while missing her sisters very much, she felt that she was beginning to let go to her distant land of Italy.

The father of dott.Calò was about sixty years old, and widowed for a long time, he was still good-looking, tall, with thick grey hair and very penetrating green eyes. He was quite taciturn, but observed everyone very carefully and often his gaze rested on Giulia. She was embarrassed and could not help but lower her eyes: she was not accustomed to the looks of men and was ashamed of her inevitable blushing cheeks. One day, while she had gone to the market of the "*Medina*" with the children and Mrs.Cordier, she had glimpsed from afar the figure of Calò's father mingling into the crowd, she followed him with a glimpse and saw that he was entering one of those small doors. She said nothing to Mrs. Cordier. She didn't want to seem curious, anyhow the fact was a little strange to her: hardly no European had access to those doors.

Shortly after Giulia learned from Mrs. Cordier that there was an Italian family in which a young mother had died leaving a small daughter and elderly parents who desperately needed help. Everyone knew that Giulia had sisters in Italy and did not hesitate to consider that surely if they came to Tunis, they would have been well behaved like Giulia.

Giulia began to think about this perspective, she thought how nice it would have been to have a member of her family there in Tunis to talk to and share so many new things together. The more she thought about it and the more she saw her sister Maria suited for that family. But how could she detach her from Carruba? This she just didn't know.

Summer was now near. The days were endless. The search for a wisp of air was made spasmodic every day. Giulia often bathed the head of the children during the day because they were the ones most exposed to the danger of heat. The only time of day longed was in the evening, after sunset, when they would all go out and find themselves in one's courtyard or another. It was on one of those evening that Giulia met Rachel, the child left without a mother. She was accompanied by her father and her grandparents. While they conversed affably, she remained apart, seated in her chair with dreamy and sad eyes. Giulia noticed that among many things Rachel resembled her sister Angiolina. Giulia felt great tenderness for that little girl in need of so much love and affection. In that moment Giulia could only think about Maria: she was the only one that could have filled that void. This is when she decided to write to Don Ettore to explain everything she had in her heart and how only he could mediate with Carruba.

On a hotter night than usual Giulia was awakened by a nightmare in her sleep: she found herself all wet with perspiration and could no longer recover her sleep. She got up slowly trying not to make a sound in order not wake anyone in the house, took an old towel and went to seek refreshment on the terrace-roof. The floor still emanated the heat absorbed during the day. Giulia stretched out her towel to the ground.

Lying on that warm floor and looking at the stars up above her she found herself asleep. She awoke suddenly with a dark figure beside her. She could not distinguish his face. She was still sleepy but she could feel his breath on her neck since he was so close. She jumped up on her feet and noticed that she had her nightgown unbuttoned that let a part of her breast be glimpsed. While going backward, she recognized that face: it was Calò's father looking at her without emitting a sound. Giulia ran away.

That episode left her a great dismay inside her heart. Then followed many days full of sadness. Every time she crossed Calò's father she changed direction or room. At last the news arrived that Maria had accepted to leave for Tunis and would arrive on early October. Don Ettore had done a great work of persuasion with Carruba. Giulia sent him out a note with a simple "thank you". He would have understood.

Maria was the most cultured and religious of the sisters. All of them had been in school and they knew how to read and write, but only she would continue her passion to write for the following years to everyone giving all advice and exhorting to pray. Accepting to leave for Tunis was dictated by the need she had heard in Giulia more than her own. Maria was very sensitive to the needs of others which often prepended to her own, she used to say:

"*if the Lord wants this, let his will be done*" or when her sisters asked how to find solutions to everyday problems, she would answer:

"*ask the Lord and pray, he will show you the way.* " She was younger than Giulia only by two years, but, despite her appearance, her character made her seem much older and mature: she was often mistaken for being the oldest.

Maria was soon well received by all, but in particular by Rachel with whom she established immediately a good relationship and a bond that lasted all her life, even when the events of both divided them forever. Maria did everything she could to be a mother and even more considering she wasn't yet; but evidently her strong sense of maternity was already latent. In the morning she would accompany Rachel to school at the "*Goulette*" where half of the Italian population that had arrived during the past years lived. Then, at home, she helped Rachel with her homework and in the evening, before she slept, she would teach her the various prayers she well knew.

Giulia finally had someone to talk with and told Maria everything about the strange situation now created between herself and Calò's father. After that episode on the roof, he looked at her differently. His glances, before distrustful and austere, had now become languid and persistent. Giulia was ever more embarrassed and tried to meet him as little as possible. Maria also suggested that she avoid that man because she did not like him at all.

The "Bardo" neighborhood was in a great expansion. The French conquest had begun a great development of public works especially in construction and in the creation of transport infrastructures. The demand for specialized labour had resulted in a real exodus of Italian workers for Tunis, most of the work done for the French colonization was undertaken by the Italians. In those days construction sites were almost everywhere building for Arab and the richer French. The incoming Italians had assumed a genuine wave of immigration that would soon change the landscape of the city forever.

One morning Maria was awaken by the noise of men speaking down the yard, looking from the window she saw that a piece of the garden wall had fallen. The workers across the street for the construction of a new villa had pulled down an old tree with very long roots that unfortunately had invaded the nearby garden and, in tearing it down, a piece of wall had come down. Maria could not understand what they were saying, perhaps they spoke in Arabic language. Rachel's father was there among them: he had integrated well and in addition to the Arabic language he also spoke discreetly French. He was there with three pretty old men and two young good-looking trying to find a solution for what had happened. Rachel called Maria, It was time to prepare for school.

A few days later, as she was returning home with Giulia, she noticed as she was approaching the house two young men sitting on the wall of the garden: one lit a cigarette to the other that in the meantime was staring at Maria. The two sisters had to pass under them and Maria remembered their faces: they were the two young workers she had seen from the window. Giulia was impressed by one of them but said nothing.

Thus for Maria began a period in which every morning she was awakened by those workers who between mixing the cement sang Arabic and Sicilian songs and when she looked out of the window she would always meet the young men's eyes. Sometimes she met one of them while returning with Rachel from school, he would be sitting there on the wall taking a break before going home, smoking a cigarette.

One day that young man took courage and talked to Maria with a very polite form using third person, *"may"* and *"could"*. At that time it was custoMaria to have a lot of respect in talking to a woman even when they became husband and wife. He presented himself as Salvatore Santonocito born in Palermo on 1893, almost the same year as Maria, born on 1894. Salvatore's parents had arrived with the great emigration from Sicily some years earlier. Angelo, his father, was a Fisherman and Giuseppa Lo Verde, his mother, took care of the house and children. Those surname made Maria laugh so much that she could scarcely restrain herself. She tried to pronounce them again but each time she would say them differently since she was only accustomed to Tuscan surnames. Salvatore got raged with her, jumped down the wall and, saying quickly goodbye, ran away.

Maria was disturbed by the incident. For many days after, she kept on thinking how she could have behaved in that way, she had always been sympathetic and polite with everyone, so she realized that she had offended that young man with her laughter. She confided this to Giulia which tried to console her, but Maria was very sad, also because it took a long time for them to meet again.

Giulia every Sunday went to Mass in the Italian church of the *"Goulette"*. Once, at the end of the celebration, she asked the priest if he knew someone as a dressmaker for Mrs. Cordier. The priest presented her two Sicilian girls: they were called Francesca and Rosina and they were sisters. Giulia and the two girls immediately became friends, so she began to visit them often at their home bringing clothes to be repaired. One day she saw Salvatore in the corridor, she had never met him before there so she was greatly surprised. While conversing with the two sisters she found out that the girls were the sisters of Salvatore and Francesco, the young men who had remained impressed in her mind since she last saw him sitting on the wall near home, they were the bricklayers.

Giulia informed Maria on who she had seen but Maria did not want to show her interest while Giulia wanted at all costs to see Francesco again. She did not live very close to Maria so she could not see them working as she did, so, when the invitation came from the girls for the evening, Giulia wanted to bring Maria with her at all cost.

That evening was particularly warm even though the autumn was now near. Arriving at the house, they saw a small group of people sitting outside on the chairs and nearby steps. Everyone was there, when Salvatore saw Maria he greeted her with a piercing look while she exchanged with her innate calmness. The speeches of that evening reviewed the dead relatives and those still alive in Sicily. Salvatore took up the issue on the surname again being very proud about his origins, he wanted to clarify this with Maria. He began by describing the origins of the surname Santonocito, narrating that after the eruption of the volcano Etna in 496 B.C., the course of the river Amenano was struck by the lava and consequently formed a very deep lake with a circumference of 6 Km. It was one of the most beautiful and enchanting places Catania was able to boast until 1600: it was surrounded by small hills and on its banks rose enchanting villas, meeting point of the brilliant people of Catania. That artificial lake was called Lake Anicito (afterwhich called Nicito).

The lake was completely destroyed and disappeared after the terrible eruption of Volcano Etna on 1669. After destroying numerous small villages, the lava stream headed for Catania and invaded the countryside and valley of Anicito pouring itself into the lake filled it up in a short time.

In the story described by Salvatore, Maria had the sensation of being in front of a very proud man for his country and his origins and this brought to mind her father and the family she had left in Italy, a veil of sadness pervaded her. Giulia, throughout the story, had often looked at Francesco, but he had not noticed her because he was absorbed in talking to a young woman sitting next to him. Intrigued by the female figure, she asked for information to the girls and, as if she had been stabbed, she learned that it was Francesco's wife: her name was Crocifissa Giudice, also Sicilian.

It was a long time since she had felt such a great pain, perhaps it was from the time of her father's death. She felt the air was missing and wanted to escape. She could barely stay where she was standing. She had to forget that boy immediately, but she still did not know how hard it would have been.

She tried to pay attention to a conversation that was going on among the older persons, when she heard the name "*Medina*" and paid attention to what they were saying. They talked about some of the local Sicilian that had taken the habit of going in certain houses hidden between clothes and colored stalls where there lived some young ladies and eunuchs who sold their bodies for money.

To Giulia came to mind Calò's father, she had seen him at the market of the "*Medina*", so this is what he was there for, she thought, but she did not say anything to anyone.

At the end of the evening Salvatore approached Maria to greet her and informed her that he would shortly leave for Italy to fight against the Austrians. The war between Italy and Austria had just broken out, and he felt the duty to serve the homeland, while his brother Francesco would remain at home with his parents. Salvatore asked Maria to wait for him and on his return, if she had felt the same way for him he would have wanted to marry her. Maria was surprised and bewildered by his firmness and frankness, she felt the pain of the imminent loss and joy at the same time for the marriage proposal. Maybe in that instant she realized that she loved that young man and said immediately yes: she would have waited for him.

On the 24th of May 1915 Italy had declared war to Austria, not for commercial interest and not craving for dominance but for the same ideals of nationality, freedom and justice that had inspired the previous patriots. Salvatore was forced to fight, for over three and a half years, a typically alpine war, on rock and ice stations at over 3000 meters of altitude, in very difficult environmental and climatic conditions especially for him who was born in Palermo and then immigrated to Tunis where he had always lived in the sun. Just living at those heights constituted a huge problem that perhaps he had underestimated: the winter lasted an average of eight months uninterrupted with heavy snowfalls from October to May; the implacable cold, oscillated in that period from – 10 °C to – 15 °C with night peaks up to – 20 °C and over. In this "white hell" the Italian Alpine and Austrian soldiers, in addition to fighting among themselves, had to survive the dangerous environmental conditions, including the implacable avalanches that, in proportion, caused more victims than the actual fighting.

Salvatore was enlisted as a gunner. The transport of cannons and machine guns in altitude was through the aid of mules, after the metal parts had been disassembled as much as possible. Wood and food was loaded on the sledges drawn by dogs. The main work to be done between one attack and the other was constituted by the construction of fortifications, barracks and paths, lairs and the laying down of barbed wire.

At the beginning of the campaign the troops passed the old border, winning the first resistances and bringing the fight to enemy territory, but soon they stopped coming across the fortified lines that the Austrian had prepared since a long time and which formed a powerful bulwark from Trentino to Carso. A few weeks were enough for Salvatore and the other companions to turn off the initial enthusiasm. Thousands of soldiers like him had enlisted volunteers for the sake of homeland, but soon they all understood the harsh reality of a fierce conflict, lacking the slightest respect for human life. From the battle of the *"Marne"* onward, the Great War lost its momentum and took hold a parallel line of trenches dug into the ground to protect themselves from enemy attack.

Salvatore found himself constantly living with the spectre of death. In the interminable hours of idleness, committed to creating, as far as possible, the semblance of a normal daily life, danger was always lurking. A sniper or a grenade broke that monotony, putting a great strain on everyone's nerves.

Whistling of the officers that ordered the assault on enemy lines would take over, by hundred they threw themselves with the bayonet grafted against the enemies; many fell like flies, mowed by machine guns, destined to bleed to death amid atrous suffering without the possibility of help because the space between the two lines of trenches represented the so-called *"nobody's land"*, an area that was banned to all rescuers.

Salvatore lost so many companions to whom he was fond of or just simply knew them for having seen them around, nevertheless their absence left the sweet memory of a joke or a smile. They continued to die just for the conquest of a few meters of land without the possibility of escape and with the awareness of going to the slaughter, to the barrage, for the foolish orders of some commander who from far away imparted orders without criterion. Shortly, Salvatore understood that the two opposing sides were confronted without being able to prevail on each other. Tormented by the cold weather and hunger, equipped with inadequate clothes, Salvatore lived buried by a sea of mud; lying down to rest was practically impossible and getting up meant exposing oneself to the fire of enemy snipers who were firing mercilessly. In this condition, hygiene was very precarious: the mice and the lice became soon inseparable companions.

In order to escape this *"scenario"*, some companions had been willing to do everything, to self-harm, to mutilate themselves or to get hurt voluntarily; but soon these episodes were severely repressed, with trials before military tribunals that decree the death sentence of hundreds of young recruits. The only foothold to life for Salvatore was the sweet memory of Maria and her huge, languid eyes that had looked at him so much before the departure. Everything else was faded. He could barely remember his brothers and parents and he felt guilty about this, but Maria was his firm point to which he had to return safely. The absence of even a minimal contact with her inflicted physical pain more than the fighting.

But on a day of tranquility he saw a companion all recurved on himself, thinking he was feeling ill, he approached him and saw that he was busy writing a letter on a yellowed sheet with a butt of a pencil. He immediately felt that he had to learn how to write at all costs, at least he could tell Maria what he felt for her and how much he loved her. The young man was called Gaetano Ranieri of Turin which listened to his plead and decided to teach him. It was indeed an enterprise that lasted several months but in the end Salvatore was able to put together the words that he so much wanted to say to Maria.

It was May 1916 when the enemy with its infantry and artillery launched a massive attack with the intent of threatening the armies on the left flank. With their superiority the Austrians broke through the lines, but the epic resistance of the infantry and the alpine fighters gave the enemy a hard fight. During that battle, many of those who had become friends of Salvatore lost their lives. His friend Rainieri fell right at his feet and finding himself alone with the Lieutenant Lanfranchi they began to machine-gun wildly. The lieutenant urged Salvatore telling him that if they would have survived the attack he would have guaranteed for Salvatore the gold medal to the value.

Salvatore now seeing the imminent death arriving on the horizon and mangled by all the bodies and blood did what he had been commanded. He did not realize how much time passed but at some point the shots faded and thinned out. He was happy to be still alive and wanted to share his happiness with Lanfranchi but unfortunately he had been deadly injured, the only words he could say were those apologizing for not being able to witness all; he died soon after.

Salvatore was in panic and didn't know what to do. Ice cold pervaded his body to the point of making him believe he would die in an instant; but he heard voices coming towards him and this shook him from his disbelief. He hid among the corpses of his friends pretending he was dead too. It was the only way to survive he thought. In fact the Austrians, passing by did not ensure on who was still alive or not, they believed that the intense cold would have done the rest on who still was alive.

He was found days later by a patrol of Alpine soldiers, almost frozen and hungry. It took him almost a month to recover, but he was sturdy and his young physique allowed him to be dispatched again this time on the *Asiago plateau*. It was June 1918 and the troops were attacked with unprecedented violence, the enemy managed to pass some positions advancing by a few kilometers, but everywhere was a counterattack, and a bulletin of those days reported; *"From the Montello to the sea, the defeated enemy, pressed by our valiant troops, crossed the Piave in disarray."*

After the serious defeat suffered, the Austrian were no longer able to take the initiative of operations. Salvatore had made new friends even though every now and then, the thought went to all those boys less than twenty year old which had lost their lives so atrociously. Ranieri, who so lovingly had taught him to write, thanks to him, he could now write to Maria even though he always omitted the horror of war and spoke only of his heart and the love that had been growing inside for all that time spent at war.

The final blow came with the battle that took the name of *Vittorio Veneto*, the offensive, broke the enemy front, in a few days overwhelmed the Austrian resistance and our columns penetrated in *Trentino and Venezia Giulia*. On the 4th of November, the Austrian command signed the armistice. After 41 month the war was over; it had cost Italy 600,000 deaths and a million of mutilated and wounded; an entire generation had sacrificed themselves.

Chapter 3: Wedding Bandini-Santonocito

On March 1919 in the Church of the *Sacred Heart (Sacré-Coeur)* of the *Bardo* in *Tunis,* Maria and Salvatore were married. Maria was accompanied at the altar by her sister Giulia being the only relative she had with her in Tunis. The wedding dress was lent to her by the father of little Rachel. He had told her that it would have been an honor for him to see her in that dress that had been of his wife and Maria had accepted gratefully. The dress was beautiful.

Rachel was one of the bridesmaid, but it took several days before convincing her: she had not taken well the idea that Maria would have gone to live elsewhere and could no longer see her as often she wanted, even though Maria had assured her that her house would always be open for her. In Italy the news of the wedding had been greeted with extreme enthusiasm by both Cherubina and her sisters even if the displeasure of not being there was great.

Elettra wrote a beautiful letter with greetings from all including Don Ettore.

For Giulia that day was one of the saddest: she was happy for her sister, but sitting in church next to Francesco and his wife Crocifissa was a torture. Throughout the celebration she could not help but repeat the words of the Priest and watching Francesco dreamed with her eyes open that she was getting married to him. When her eyes crossed those of Crocifissa... the dream vanished.

Inside the church, to attend the celebration, also the Calò family was there. The professor had remained at the end of the church kneeling beside a pedestal of lighted candles that illuminated his face highlighting the look that seemed to be sunk in nothing and little attentive to what was going on.

Salvatore and Maria were radiant. She had waited so long for him between tears and prayers. There had not been much time to know each other before his departure, but thanks to his letters, love had grown with distance and, since Salvatore had returned, they had discovered to have a strong understanding, the words were not necessary, at a glance they could understand each other on everything. Maria would have wanted to know more about what had happened at war, his experiences, his feelings, but she had seen a veil of sadness dropping on his eyes every time that topic was mentioned. For this reason those years at war were stored in the memory, and only years later, he would share some episodes in order to evoke some anecdote about a companion or a place.

Salvatore had found two rooms for rent from a wealthy Jew-Frenchman named Zass to whom he had built a beautiful mansion in the vicinity of the *"Goulette"*. He had worked also during the night in order to finish on time and Zass had been grateful for this. Now he could not deny that rent at his conditions, he would have paid from time to time when he had the money and not at a fixed deadline. Salvatore knew how to deal with everyone: Arabs, Italians, a little less with French, rich and poor. He had a natural charm and a sympathy that attracted everyone, as well as being a great worker. Francesco although being his brother, was more conservative and reserved.

Salvatore was known by all as "*Soveur*". He had arrived from Sicily as a child, grown up with the Arabs, had a deep respect for their culture, spoke the Arabic language as them and for this was accepted and respected. The environment was multiracial, but everyone remained together according its breed and there was no possibility of interacting or even less familiarize with mixed marriages etc.

Perhaps it was the job as a bricklayer that made him be in contact for the majority with Arabs, all day side by side, mortar and bricks under that scorched sun where everyone drank from the same jug and exchanged cigarettes until dinner time. Simple people where political ideals were not mentioned and the religion of others was respected while not spoken.

After a year their first son was born and they called him Angelo as the father of Salvatore. The tradition among the Sicilian to pass on the name of the grandfather was strong and often within the same family group all were called with the same name.

Finally summer came again. Giulia was now a grown up woman and many were the suitors who asked to make her acquaintance, but she promptly refused any kind of proposal. She knew she had to forget Francesco, he was married and did not even notice her, but it was hard for her. That summer something had to happen that would have changed her life forever and would put the word end on Francesco.

In July Mrs. Cordier together with her husband departed for France. They had not seen their relatives for a long time and they in return had not seen the children since they were born, it would have been a good opportunity to get away from that scorching heat. They would only return in late August. Giulia had to stay in Tunis to take care of the house and Prof. Calò that unfortunately had not departed with them.

This new situation had made Giulia a little embarrassed but fortunately she would only see him at meals, then he was nowhere to be found and to her this was more than desired. That man had always given her a seemingly inexplicable sense of discomfort. The evening at dinner they ate one in front of the other without even saying a word. At the end of the meal he would get up, say good night and retire to his room. One evening Giulia was almost worried since it was dinner time, but Prof. Calò had not yet returned. She had the habit of waiting for him, she thought it might be polite from her side. Upon his return he sat down at the table without even looking at her, she approached him and served the meal and immediately felt a strong odor of alcohol coming from his clothes. Strangely that evening he poured wine into her glass, which he had never done before. Giulia did not know what to do, she did not have the habit of drinking wine, but did not want to seem rude by denying. She accepted without saying a word. During the entire dinner he did nothing else but drink and gave Giulia threatening glances when he looked at her glass and realized that the girl was not drinking. She felt instigated to drink against her own will and he continued to fill her glass until the end of the meal, then he got up staggered to the door and gave her good night.

Giulia retired in her room. She was very hot that so she undressed and remained in her nightgown lying on the bed, the windows slightly open to get some fresh air in that particular night with such a stuffy heat. She was in the dark, but the moonlight entered the room and created strange shadows with the few furniture present. The door was slightly open when a noise attracted Giulia's gaze towards that direction; standing in front of her was Prof. Calò who was staring at her with a strange light in his eyes almost like fire, he had his mouth half-opened. Giulia remained petrified, unable to move any muscle; only her mind travelled fast, she saw all the moments she had previously had with the Prof., and while he was lowering down almost to touch her face, she remembered the words of Maria telling her not to give too much confidence to that man, then her mother Carruba and the little sisters, finally the sweet eyes of Francesco and then..... nothing else.

He was above her like a pounding dog he tore her nightgown; she tried with her humble forces to rebel, but he had the strength of an angry wolf and Giulia was unable to oppose the violence she suffered. The dawn was outside her window and woke her up from the amazement in which she had been for who knows how many hours. The girl tried to get up but nearly fainted on seeing her white blood-soaked nightgown. Then she burst into an inconsolable cry for the shame that she felt almost as if it had been her fault to be in that condition. She prepared herself to go out. She didn't know what to do, but she certainly wanted to escape from that house. Lucky enough she didn't meet him. She rushed to Maria's house, which, once informed on what had happened, began weeping with her and started to pray all the saints.

Behind the advice of Maria, the two sisters wrote a note for Prof. Calò: Giulia informed him that because of the birth of her nephew Angelo she had to help her sister for a period that would be protracted until the return of Mrs Cordier. She didn't have to make the slightest hint of what had happened, it would have remained a family secret. Maria had learnt well the Sicilian customs transmitted by Salvatore, namely, the honor of the family above all things and to omit at all costs.

Unfortunately their plan remained only a good intention; they didn't know at that time that Giulia was expecting a child and this would have changed many things. In fact, on the return of Mrs. Cordier the two sisters were forced to inform her also because soon she would have seen her belly get bigger and had to agree a plan together.

They cried all together and after many hours they came to the decision that would have protected Giulia more but also the entire family Cordier. The secret remained between the three women and the name of the father was never revealed. Giulia had to return to Italy, to the Pinewoods of Fucecchio, to Carruba (for health reasons was told to everyone that asked) where she gave birth to a male son to whom she gave her surname, Bandini. Only a few years later she would return to Tunis.

Chapter 4 – Angelo and his short life

Angelo Santonocito was born on the 19th of January 1919; Angelo by name and nature. He was born with very blond hair so much that Salvatore was almost ashamed to show this son around that little resembled him, while for Maria this had no meaning at all, from the beginning she had a strong feeling with him. As he began to walk, Angelo followed her almost everywhere: he was her shadow, and never cried.

His name was never pronounced: it was enough to look at the feet of Maria and he was there ready to follow her on every step. When grown up, he would always be ready to offer his help to Maria for the heavier duties. Salvatore often would try to take him with him in order to start him at his own job, but he would point out that his help was necessary to Maria, who in a short time after him had given birth to two other children: Giuseppina who was born on the 23rd of September 1920 and Candido on the 19th of November 1923.

The close birth of these children had put Maria's body to a hard task. Fortunately she could count on the help of Rosina and Francesca, the sisters of Salvatore who often came to her home and looked after the children, since Giulia had returned to Italy,

Maria felt more lonely inwardly despite her children and her husband.

Growing up, Angelo showed more and more a keen interest on mechanics instead of as a bricklayer like Salvatore had wished. Next to their house there was an Italian mechanic who adjusted everything: from cars to bicycles, to agricultural tools, etc. Angelo used to run there in his spare time and soon the owner entrusted him with small duties that he rewarded with some coins. Angelo was really gifted for fixing everything and soon his true passion became that of electronics and everything related to that.

In Tunis, the era of the Fascism began at the end of the twenties and ended after about ten years incorporating all the Italian institutions existing on the Tunisian territory. The school institutions, which became propaganda centers along with cultural circles, sports associations, and the hospital, passed under the Fascism control. From these structures were excluded all those who were not enrolled in the National Fascism Party (NFP). In Italy, the *coup d'état* by the Fascism, with the "March on Rome" of 1922, culminated with the nomination of Benito Mussolini as the new Prime Minister. Salvatore had no sympathy for Fascism, in fact he was pro-socialism, but would never make comments at home and especially when outside. The spies of the NFP were everywhere and a word to the Italian Console was enough not to make you find a job. Even Angelo, while attending school, could not sympathize with the Fascism and he also abstained on giving judgments. At home reigned the most absolute silence concerning political matters.

Apart from the love he had for his mother Maria, Angelo had a very strong feeling with his sister Giuseppina who everyone called Pina. Among them, only a year difference and growing together they had shared everything. He confided to her those little things that he could not tell Maria, and the same was true for her. Maria had conveyed her strong Christian faith also to her children and especially to Angelo, who would never have dared to contradict her in anything, while from the mouth of Salvatore some blasphemy words escaped especially when he was tired from work. Maria at that point would raise her eyes and with a glance, which only he understood, would become mild and change his mood.

Angelo grew up quickly and Maria was dismayed by the clothes that were no longer suitable after a few months. As a remedy she would pass them to Candido who was smaller about four years, but for Angelo she was forced to use the trousers of Salvatore making a greater hem at the end that would be lowered as time passed by. This was the only way to solve the clothing problem. At sixteen Angelo was already up a meter and ninety, a rarity for that time where the average height for men, including Salvatore, was scarcely a meter and seventy. Only he would be so tall in the family, the other males would have stopped at one meter and eighty. The children in the area who knew him, called him the good giant, he often put himself on his knees to play with them in the yard, they would do everything but he never lost his patience and if Pina did not arrive to free him from them he would remain there for hours.

Around the end of the '20s, Salvatore felt a strong need to return to Italy due also to the fact that he had met a wealthy businessman from Milan who had much appreciated his way of working, especially the first works done in reinforced concrete of which he built various villas.

The idea of returning to Italy did not mind at all to Maria; she would have the opportunity to see her mother and sisters and make them meet her children. Salvatore also tried to convince his brother Francesco to go to Milan, but he did not succeed, he was now rooted in Tunis and for him Milan was a city much too cold. For the first time, Salvatore separated himself from his brother. The temporary separation occurred in 1928.

The period spent in Milan, strangely enough, was for Maria the happiest of all her life, she would talk about it often even years later. Angelo was nine years old, Pina eight and Candido five.

After 1929 the imperial expansion became one of the favourite themes of Benito Mussolini's fascist government aspiring to the reconstruction of an empire, in the style of the Roman's. He had put his eyes on Abyssinia in Africa, the only state, together with Liberia, still independent, and therefore its eventual invasion was not going to provoke, in theory, any international intervention.

Besides the proximity to Eritrea to the east and Italian Somalia to the south, they could determine the creation of an important area of Italian influence. On the 3rd of October 1935, 100,000 Italian soldiers under the command of Marshal Emilio De Bono began to advance from their bases in Eritrea.

Ethiopia (Abyssinia was once called the northern part) was a country as vast as Italy, France, Switzerland, Austria and Belgium all together. It occupied most of Cape Horn, the easternmost region of the continent, between the Red Sea and the Indian Ocean. Icy mountains, beyond four thousand meters, torrid plains, an impressive landscape, with peaks, deep gorges, jagged rocks, and the mountains that most characterize it, the "Ambe", cones with the top cut flat, volcanoes and lakes, especially in the long rift, the Great Rift Valley, which from north-east Ethiopia descends to Mozambique.

A melting pot of people (one of the possible etymologies of Abyssinia is "mixture"), of language, custom and religion. The Fascist soldiers stationed in

Tunis began to rake among the young Italians to persuade them to go and fight for their homeland in Abyssinia. Some were fervently accepting; others were obliged to accept as in the case of Angelo.

Returned to Tunis from Milan with his parents, brother and sister in 1931, Angelo had resumed working as a mechanic in the usual workshop, next to his house, where he had made his apprenticeship from childhood. In that distant 1935, Angelo, just sixteen-year-old, had made himself some regular clients even among the French and the Arabs. He was a hard worker, and the enthusiasm to work came from the joy he felt when he put in his mother's hands the money he had earned. For him happiness consisted mainly in the help he could give to his family.

Angelo's skill, as an expert electronic technician, was also noted by the NFP members. Some persons reported to the Fascist military leaders of Tunis saying:

"The sixteen-year-old Angelo Santonocito should be placed on the list of those ready to leave for Abyssinia. He's a good mechanic and an electronic technician, he will be a very useful element for our army".

Angelo was summoned to the Command, but, since he was born in Tunis, he could only enlist as a "volunteer"; everyone else born in Italy for example had the obligation to enlist. For this reason Angelo Santonocito was forced to enlist to save his father

Salvatore from unpleasant retaliation. Angelo never revealed to his family what had happened at the Command, he made all believe that he had enlisted voluntarily. Only his sister Pina knew the whole truth.

Salvatore was very surprised at the choice of his son, but he approved the decision remembering how he had made the same choice to participate in the 1st World War. For Maria instead it was a great pain, he was just a boy she thought, that for the first time would have been away from her. She tried to stifle the pain down in her heart in order not to make it noticeable to others.

Candido, the twelve-year-old brother, was desperate, but only because he wanted to follow his brother: he was his hero the one to imitate at all cost. Apart from this there was also a hint of envy because Angelo was called to do a great thing and everyone would talk about him for months. Being the smallest, he was often not considered in the choices of the family nor questioned. He had a great admiration for his elder brother but, at the same time, he did not feel loved or regarded as him by the others especially by his mother, and this sense of frustration went to fortify his strong and rebellious character which he already had by nature.

The war lasted only a few months and the victory was officially communicated by Mussolini to the Italian people on the evening of the 5th of May 1936. Angelo would return home without even firing a shotgun, thanks to the fact that he had been placed in a camp as a telegrapher.

One of Angelo's passion was to play the harmonica, in his spare time he would go and sit on the branch of the only tree they had in the garden and there he would escape into his own silent world. One day, looking down on the street from up there, he saw a young girl who had stopped on the sidewalk to listen to him, she gave Angelo a smile and ran away. On more than one occasion this girl would be seen in front of the house as if waiting for him.

Pina noticed her and asked Angelo for explanations, joking about it. The girl was the daughter of another family also from Palermo who lived in front of them and with whom the Salvatore had repeatedly "argued" for work reason with the father. One day, timidly, Angelo asked his mother what she thought of that girl, it was the first time he talked about a girl with her and unfortunately it would have been the only one, many times after that episode for all her life Maria regretted giving her answer.

Maria had confined herself by saying that she had not too much sympathy for that girl perhaps because of the dissensions with the family. For Angelo those words from his mother were enough for him to drop the subject and stopped playing the harmonica in the garden forever in order not to attract the girl. He never touched that argument again.

On the 10th of June 1940, day of the declaration of War of our country with France, marked the end of the state of privilege of the Italian community in Tunisia. About 25,000 Italians were sent to concentration camps in Tunis. In those camps everything was present, from Fascist persons to none, intellectual and poor. As the war went on, these camps were filled with Italian soldiers captured in the various battles and sent down here. Here began the death of many soldiers: someone for sickness, someone killed by the machine guns of the Tunisian guards. The Gaullists hated to death the Italians: they said that we had stabbed them in the back with the declaration of war, that Mussolini had attacked the French by opening the hostilities on the Western Front and the poor Italian military suffered the consequences. When some Italian soldier was killed by the Tunisian guards, they justified themselves with the pretext of the stab behind the back of 1940, it was, in short, a revenge that was practiced day by day against those poor soldiers.

In this context happened that many Italians became the spies of the French, in order to get some more attention: they were spying on those families who had some men enlisted in the army in their homeland. Candida was now a volunteer in the "Folgore" as a paratrooper. Unnecessarily, Salvatore tried to explain to him that his enlistment would endanger the entire family. Not even Maria's prayers were of any help. Candido was very obstinate, for much too long he had wanted to assert himself, he had remained in the shadow of the brother that everyone adored. Finally the opportunity had come to demonstrate something and not so much for his political ideals but for his courage in defending the homeland.

One evening after dinner the French militia knocked at Salvatore's door to lead him to the command. They said they wanted to ask him questions about his son Candido. Maria felt almost like fainting, but she made herself courage for her younger children. Angelo wanted to go with him, but he was denied permission. In the following days unfortunately things did not get any better, the French decided to send Salvatore in a concentration camp.

Angelo opposed himself with all his strength and declared willing to take his father's place, relying on the fact that his father still had two little children to support while Angelo had no family of his own. The militia at the end accepted and Angelo was sent to a French concentration camp called "*La Marsa*".

More than a concentration camp it was a field of forced labor. The youngest and strongest were employed for the reconstruction of roads, while the weaker ones were employed in the cultivation of the fields. Angelo found himself splitting the shack with 20 other men, they had to work more than ten hours a day, in the evening, after the meal, Angelo collapsed from exhaustion. The wooden cabins in the daytime were impregnated with heat but in the evening they returned the heat in humidity. As a result of sweat, moisture and bacteria, the shack became a receptacle place for many diseases.

In addition the shortage of food made everyone weak even the stronger, Angelo resisted almost two years to all this. Then he was sent home when a terrible fever took hold of him supposing a strong pneumonia well in advance. Maria almost fainted at the sight of him when he arrived home, he was exhausted and could hardly speak he only emitted weak lamentations which made all present shudder.

Pina was barely able to support her mother when she herself wished to be sustained, but she couldn't give up right now. And she took courage. Pina, who had always shared everything with Angelo, she felt part of him, not only his sister, but his mother, his best friend, and now he was going to abandon her. The younger brothers looked at him and cried. They did not understand what was going on, but in the air the sentence was clear, something terrible would happen shortly.

When Angelo left home for the concentration camp, he left behind his beloved dog named Diana. The dog at the sight of his master, laid down next to his bed and there he remained for all the following days without seeking neither food nor water. Angelo's eyes lit up at the sight of his mother and wanted to ask her for pasta with the ricotta that he loved so much. Maria prepared that dish with all the love she had for him knowing inside herself that it would have been the last. After a few hours the heart of Angelo ceased to beat and a beautiful smile seized his young face. He looked like an angel. He was only 25 years old, it was 1945.

For days and days the dog lying next to the empty bed, emitted hisses of lamentation that seemed almost human and made the hearts of those who listened mangle. There was no way to make her move from that place until one day they found her lying on a side without breathing. She seemed to smile also, maybe she was happy because she finally could reach Angelo.

Praise to Memory

On the white houses
echoing the chimes, for alleys goes
death covered with a garland of whitered
Jasmine flowers.
It plays and plays a resigned song with
its ivory guitar.
I watched him closely, his beautiful body
lying on the bed, still warm,

as a throbbing mineral he refused
to cool down, his eyes were open,
as if not wanting to depart from his
young life. He was holding his hands
tight, as if to keep a hold on his last dreams.
From under the bed two
phosphorescent eyes leaking
of incessant lamentations, the faithful
dog fills the funeral room.
The lashing wind outside
chokes the dear Mother's weeping,
and the fine sand builds sepulchral dunes.
On the white tower of the
church the bells are muting.

*Poem written by Umberto Santonocito, dedicated to
his brother Angelo, who died for the madness of Men.
Tunis 1945.*

Chapter 5 – The twins

On returning to Tunis from the time spent in Milan Italy, Maria discovered that she was pregnant again and from what she said to the nanny they would surely have been two children. For Maria, every child was a blessing from God and despite the scarce economic conditions in which she lived, she could not despair, but only see the mysterious side of love. Salvatore saw it quite differently and regretted it even though he could not do anything about it. At that time the births were hardly programmed, but rather suffered by both men and women. Pina was ten years old and she already felt like a little woman, she liked to help her mother and was good at school, the game had been abandoned early. In the house there was always so much to do and she felt she had to help her mother, especially now that she saw the womb of her mother grow and her forces become less, so in the evening she and Angelo had determined to divide the homework for what they could.

The tragic day came when on a Sunday morning everyone went to the beach to the "*Goulette*" in order to stay a few hours. It was a particularly hot and humid day and Salvatore decided to take his children to swim with him, he was a very experienced swimmer and as a result the first thing he had taught them since they were born, was swimming. Pina was the best and swam like a fish, she loved to follow him as far as she could. It was a wonder to see that little girl so reckless. The beach was not particularly busy that morning and Maria had found herself a place near the water where she could see her kids swimming. The light sea breeze stroked her hair and she could already hear the kicks of the twins in her womb. She was in her fifth month. Candido, already as a child, was rather rebellious and when she told him to do something he used to do the opposite, he wanted to imitate the older brothers, but inevitably he was not able to, he had a temper and character all of his own, he was different from the others.

The initial calm sea had gradually become rippled and Salvatore had already asked everyone several times to get out of the water. The boys hesitated a little as always and Pina was the first to get out of the water, the others soon followed. Candido continued to remain far from the shore, not taking care that the others had already gone out. The waves were slowly taking him further on, no one noticed anything in the roar of the chatter and laughter when, at some point, Maria, looking out on the open sea, saw Candido floundering in the waves and then disappearing underwater. Her cry of despair made everyone on the beach turn towards the direction in which she was looking and it took a little for Salvatore to understand what had happened. With a leap he plunged into the water and swam to the utmost of his forces, he managed to reach Candido, who in the meantime had returned to the surface. He took him from behind by putting his arm under his neck and always swimming took him to the shore. There they remained exhausted almost breathless, while the people, coming from all directions, had gathered around Maria who seemed to be fainting. Everyone told her that Candido had been rescued by Salvatore and that he was fine, but she could not get out of her eyes the scene of Candido that was going down swallowed by the waves. Pina, who had witnessed all this had remained still without the slightest movement only her heart was pounding in her breast.

In the following days Maria began to have a blood leak and more intense uterine contractions to the point of having to call the midwife. Upon her arrival, immediately she realized the seriousness of the situation, by now she could not hear the heartbeat of the twins and the contractions had dilated the neck of the uterus. She had to intervene immediately. There was no time to take her to the nearest hospital she ordered boiling water and rags to Salvatore, then looking at Pina, she told her to be strong because she would have needed her help.

Maria gave birth to twins, after much suffering, but they were dead. The midwife wrapped them in a towel and put them in the arms of Pina without showing them to Maria, she was too weak to support the sight. Pina was the only one in the family to see the twins as she arranged them in a shoe box which had been prepared before. She lifted the towel in order to give a peek and uttered a sigh of wonder, they were like two little dolls sleeping, candid as snow, they were two boys.

Maria was very weak after the childbirth. She had lost a lot of blood and was psychologically destroyed. The doctor often came to visit her at home and every time he advised Salvatore that absolutely she should not have any more children. Maria had no appetite, and she ate very little. Her thinness worried all the family. She began to feel better only at the news that her beloved sister Giulia was going to return to Tunis.

So many years had passed and they had never seen each other again. It would have been great to have her back. There were a lot of things to talk about. Giulia had not an easy life in Italy with a child without being married. She was often denigrated by people and men approached her only with certain intention. Now the son had grown up and there was extreme need for money. She had to work and for this she had written to Mrs. Cordier with the prayer of finding her a place among the families of her acquaintance. She would leave her son with Carruba. Giulia found work as a maid in a house of French persons, she only worked in the morning and in the afternoon had time free to help Maria with her children. She avoided on purpose to go to Mrs. Cordier's house. In agreement with her they had decided that it was better to avoid that place in order not to meet Prof. Calò. But despite all the tricks taken not to meet the Prof. the mocking destiny did the rest. One day while Giulia was walking among the stalls of the Medina market she came across with him, face to face.

She tried pretending that she hadn't recognized him, lowered her eyes and made the act of changing direction, but he grabbed her arm and in a loud voice begged her to stop. Gulia could not help noticing how he had aged, his eyes still more sunken and sad, his face very skinny, and the hand that grabbed her arm was trembling. Giulia realized that she felt sorry for that man who had ruined her life, she had hated him for a long time and now that she had him there before her she could not help to be sorry for his state. The eyes were moistened with tears that descended on his rosy cheeks. They embraced each other, and he could not finish asking her for forgiveness, forgiveness for everything, almost a confession now that he had little time to live, he was terribly ill. They left each other with the promise that she would have gone to make visit to him, but she did not have enough time, he died shortly after and never knew that Giulia had a child from him.

After a few years Maria was pregnant again despite the doctor's warnings. This new pregnancy seemed to restore her strength and vigor. She was well and happy, always interpreting everything as a blessing from the Lord. Pina saw her mother's belly grow and this reminded her of the Twins. She was afraid and didn't want to see her suffer. Maria knew what her daughter had in her heart, the nanny had told her how good she had been and how much help she had given on that occasion. So, day after day, Maria would assure her daughter that all would have gone well this time.

On the 16th of June 1932 another male was born and they called him Ferdinando Adriano. Adriano had been a dear uncle of Maria in Italy. Ferdinando had blond curly hair that while growing became almost white, everyone would think he was a girl. For a certain time Ferdinando enjoyed being the last, cuddled by Pina as a doll. She, now being a young lady, took him for walks as soon as she could and enjoyed showing him to everyone as her favorite toy. But, not even four years later, the last son of Maria and Salvatore was born; they called him Umberto Benito after the king still in force and the emerging power of Benito Mussolini. It was the 9th of March, 1936.

The great difference of age with the elder brothers meant that the events of war that followed were experienced by spectators. Small spectators who watched the horrors of war with incredulous and frightened eyes, without understanding, they suffered and were forged to what they became once grown up. The others lived as protagonist with the direct consequences on their skin without having the possibility to escape.

At first Ferdinando did not want to see the last arrived, he saw him as an invader of the position that had previously been his. In addition Pina now, had to carry around two instead of one and being grown up, she was sixteen, people would mistake her for their mother. In that period Pina had to abandon the French school she was attending, the commitments of the family caused her presence to be necessary at home. She was very intelligent at school, she studied well and it was a shame for her to stop studying, but throughout her life, the French language remained her second language. Unfortunately, after only twenty days after the birth of Umberto a letter from Italy arrived announcing the death of Cherubina. Maria was grief-stricken for the loss.

She had not been back in Italy for many years and had not been able to see her mother again. This grief chased her for a long time. The sudden and unexpected pain caused the milk she had in her for Umberto to disappear suddenly, and had to resort to the powder milk of Nestlè.

It was the first great mourning that Pina really faced. She had only seen her grandmother once in her life, when as a child she had been in Milan for the short Italian parenthesis. In spite of this she was very fond of her, Maria had much talked about her so that the children, growing up, had clear the figure and personality of the grandmother. A life was going away carrying a part of the family history along with her.

Chapter 6 – Wedding of Pina 1940

Growing up Pina had acquired a great dexterity in women's work especially on knitting and crochet. She used to do everything from sweaters, socks and scarfs. In a short time she would do any sort of work for other families as well. They commissioned her all kind of things and thus she soon began to earn her first money, which she invariably put in the house.

One day Mrs. Calamusa, which lived next door, invited her at home to talk about her daughter who was waiting her first child: she had to make a lot of knitting for the event and Pina was very happy about this. That afternoon she was wearing her light blue cotton dress with small white flowers that she adored, she wanted to make a good impression. It was spring and the sun was already burning in the clear sky while the air was soaked with the scent of jasmine flowers in bloom. Pina had long wavy black hair that sparkled in the sun. She was proud of her hair and treated them very well with vinegar on the last rinse, they had told her that they would have been more shiny, and in fact they were.

She arrived punctually for this appointment and while the young women spoke, a man entered the room. He was not very young, he must have been already in his advanced thirties, he was beginning to be bald and wore small round glasses. He sat aloof after giving a wave of greeting to Mrs. Calamusa, also present in the room, and a quick glance at Pina. Before leaving Mrs. Calamusa, presented that man to Pina as her eldest son, he was a teacher and taught at an Italian School in the *Goulette*. He was affable and had kind manners, very polite noticed Pina after he had accompanied her to the door.

In the days that followed Pina often met that man going to the house of the Calamusa. His name was Giovanni and every time she went in that house he would be present in the room where she was with his sister. Sometimes Pina took the little brothers with her and he was very kind with them, making them play and laugh. Pina gladly went to the Calamusa that seemed a very united family where everything was decided by the mother, perhaps because the father had died years earlier. Everyone in the house seemed to have accepted this condition without much trouble, and Pina spoke to Maria about this. Unfortunately in Pina's house there was not so much peace lately.

Candido was kicking to join the *"Folgore"* in Italy as a paratrooper and the money was always lacking for this large family. Fortunately with Angelo's work they managed to move forward. Salvatore lately only had occasional jobs followed by periods of rest and this made him approach alcohol which usually made him drunk in the evenings. This condition made him have guilty feelings towards Maria for the life he was making her have, which only made things worse. When he returned home at night the rage he had in his body combined with the exuberance of Candido, who was the only one in the family which would stand up at him not being afraid of his condition, would make an explosive combination. Maria and Pina with the younger brothers would retire in their rooms and pray.

Giovanni was already thirty-five when he met Pina, had his work as a teacher, was very respected and had also done well with the French because he spoke their language just like them. He had a great respect for his mother and had always accepted her advice concerning the choice of the future bride. Until then none of the chosen ones had been proper for her son and had been rejected. Now, perhaps because she saw that the age of her son was advancing or because she really liked Pina, she began to put down ideas on the possibility of a marriage for him.

He did not feel all this great desire for marriage, but did not dare go against the will of the mother and every time he saw Pina looked at her and watched her closely from head to toe trying to find the courage to declare his intentions. Pina became a little dizzy about all this attention and she got as little upset during those meetings. It was the first time a man looked at her with so much intense, it was also the first time a man showed her such kindness. Her young age did the rest, she was a mixture of sensations, never tried before, up to the point that she thought she had fallen in love with that man and that maybe she could marry him too. Then followed sleepless nights, Pina felt she was attracted to that man, but couldn't stand the idea of leaving her home. How would her mother have done without her? and her brothers? months passed and Pina was more and more convinced that despite her feelings for the family the right thing to do was to marry. In doing so she could help her family better without aggravating with one person more to feed. Mrs. Calamusa was extremely happy, at last she would see her beloved son married, therefore she stepped forward proposing to organize everything with the consent of Maria who greatly appreciated the gesture believing to give the best to her daughter.

The night before the wedding, Pina put her white dress on the chair, it was extremely simple, consisting on a skirt at her knee and blouse with a small collar. The white shoes had been borrowed from the previous marriage of his sister since she had the same number. She had asked for an old rag to Maria and had reduced it in many strips with which she had wrapped a strand at a time her thick black hair; the next day she would have untied them one by one creating the effect of a cascade of ringlets.

Pina entered the Church of the Sacred Heart (Sacré-Coeur) in 1940, in that church her parents had married years before. Salvatore accompanied her to the altar excited as ever, while he could not believe that his only daughter was getting married so young, Giovanni was already there waiting for her.

The church was illuminated mainly by candles and small light bulbs scattered here and there. The floral decoration was composed of small bouquets of white carnation Jasmine flowers that gave off a fresh and sweet scent. In this sweet atmosphere, Pina, arrived at the altar and for the first time saw who was going to be the witness from Giovanni's side. He was a young cousin that she had never seen before. He was younger than Giovanni of about a few years and his name, she learnt later was Antonio. He had thick black hair and eyes just as black.

During the entire ceremony she just could not take her eyes off him and the same was for him. Their eyes attracted each other like magnets. Pina's heart stood still for a second when it was her turn to say "*yes*". That word was glued inside her lips struggling to get out. She didn't understand what was going on really, it was as if she had woke up from a long sleep and didn't recognize the place she was in, but it was too late.

Unfortunately she could not escape. She had arrived there by her own choice and belief, she couldn't blame anyone. Pina was now married to the wrong man that she would have never loved, but still did not know fully.

Months passed, relatives came and went with the usual Sunday visits and also Antonio would often attend the house of the cousin. Pina tried not to be present when she knew he was coming because the sight of him troubled her too much, but often he would suddenly appear so for her it was torture. At a certain point, Pina felt she needed to confide with her mother about the matter.

One day she found the courage and faced her mother telling that she was still untouched by her husband since the wedding. It was true that during the entire engagement he had never looked at her in a sensual way, only gave her some light kisses on the cheek, but now they were husband and wife. Maria could hardly believe what she was hearing, she had such a dashing husband who had given her so many children, for her it was impossible to imagine anything else. She tried to comfort her daughter by telling her that maybe it was because of her young age and he only wanted to respect her and not rush things. Pina accepted her mother's advice and even felt relieved now that she had talked to someone about this, but of course mentioned nothing about Antonio. To be frank with herself she did not know whether to feel offended by her husband's negligence or to be pleased, basically she wasn't attracted to him in the physical way since she had seen Antonio for the first time in church. He had now entered her heart and gave her so many sleepless nights, she had said nothing to Maria about all this, she would not have her understanding.

Pina adored the seaside like the rest of her family and was also a good swimmer thanks to Salvatore who had taught her to swim since she was a child, while Giovanni could not swim and, despite his cousin's efforts, he didn't even want to learn. He had very white skin and could not stand the sun, he had to protect himself. One day it happened that talking about the seaside and swimming, Antonio invited Pina and Giovanni to go to Carthage.

Pina had never been there before and remained ecstatic, it would have become their favorite place years later. On the ruins of the ancient Carthage, stretched out a very charming and rich region located along the seaside with turquoise clear water like a lagoon. A succession of pretty villages, such as *La Marsa* and *Sidi Bou Said*, did the rest.

Close enough to Tunis and rich of its prestigious past, it was the preferred place of some rich Tunisian families, the Cypress and bouganville, aligned among the dazzling whiteness of the houses and in the summer the Jasmine flowers spread their essences in every corner of the streets.

They arranged Giovanni in a shelter and stripped off the clothes they wore. Pina saw the most handsome man she had ever seen. His athletic and already tanned body made a young woman like her blush. They ran on the fiery sand to the sea but did not feel the burning under their feet because their hearts were burning more, they plunged into the crystalline waters and swam to a certain distance until they had breath and stopped to see how far they were from the shore. Giovanni could hardly be seen from their distance. They were very close to each other and their hands touched while their eyes plunged into one another, then they went underwater together.

There were not many words said after that episode. At that time it was not common to talk about feelings between a man and a woman in public, they used to address to each other in third person, but with their eyes they would understand the other's feeling perfectly, in fact when they were in the presence of Giovanni they would try not to look at each other.

By now their destiny was marked, they did everything to see each other even for a few seconds, they invented excuses and found the most varied pretenses. One day, while Giovanni was at school teaching, Pina took the youngest brothers to the seaside with Antonio, in this way no one could have doubted about them. The hours passed quickly and found themselves still there at sunset.

The sun was dropping into the water throwing a long red tongue that came up to the beach. Unfortunately time was now late and there was no more public transport to take them into town. They decided to sleep there crouched inside a cave that overlooked the sea and the next day they would return home. The boys were delighted with the idea of staying outdoor under the stars and Pina had her heart leaping to her throat with emotion without thinking about who would be worried for not seeing them return. Time passed and the exhausted boys fell asleep while Pina and Antonio remained awake.

That was the longest and most exciting night of their lives. They slipped into the warm water of the night and their bodies found themselves clinging to an embrace that did not end until exhausted they laid down, on the warm sand of the day exhausted by making love and the kisses that they had given to each other.

At dawn they took the first bus that passed to return home. Strangely, no one asked anything. Maria thought that the boys had stayed to sleep at Pina's house and Giovanni thought that she had stayed at her mother's house. Pina, lost her patience that had been one of her major virtue, she became also nervous and often found herself arguing with Giovanni for small issues. Pina realized that she could never have Antonio as her husband, she was a married woman and as such adultery was conceived neither by the Sicilians nor the Arabs. In front of the community she would have been appointed as adulterous.

The situation was absurd, Pina was married to a man she didn't love and could not even hope to have children to comfort herself because he did not even touch her with a finger. She could only hope to be a secret lover to the only man she loved, without hoping for any kind of future together.

Candido had now departed to enlist in the "Folgore" despite the objections of the family members. Salvatore, in the end, had succumbed to the demands of his son and Angelo had been taken prisoner instead of him. These last events had greatly changed him and made him calmer. He drank less wine so as not to displease Maria and was much more docile to the younger children now that they were in the house. When he found Pina at home waiting for him like the old days, his heart was filled with joy. She was his little girl even though she had become a beautiful adult woman.

Looking at her carefully lately he had noticed that something troubled her. He even found her thinner and asked her often if she ate enough. He had not said anything to Maria about how he saw his daughter in order not to disturb her, but he decided to face Pina openly with what he was thinking.

With a pretext he went to her house and finding her alone took courage and asked her with his pure and beautiful Sicilian accent;

"Pina, what troubles you? doesn't your husband know how to make you happy? Why so much sadness in your eyes? And why, although some years have passed, you have no children? "

At those questions Pina failed to hold back the tears and burst into a sound hiccup. How could she lie to her father who had read her deepest sorrow at the bottom of her soul. She revealed to him that her marriage was a sad marriage because her husband had never looked at her as a wife but more like a sister, but she said nothing of her great love for Antonio, on that he would have not understood.

Salvatore was deeply disturbed and could not understand how this could happen. He wanted to take Pina away immediately from that house, but first he wanted to better understand the reason for so much indifference and why a man would get married and then neglect his wife in this way. Salvatore had many friends, mainly between the Arabs and among them was so much complicity and sympathy. Everyone understood the rules of the other and nobody interfere. Salvatore asked one of them to follow Giovanni for a certain period of time, he wanted to understand where he was going, who he was dating, if he had a lover or what else was behind his behavior without saying anything in the house, much less to Pina. After a couple of months the sad discovery came through, more painful than he could have imagined.

Giovanni was usual to visit the Medina and there he would meet with young Tunisian and then disappeared behind some doors, it was clear enough that he was homosexual. Salvatore had to say everything to his daughter and Pina was devastated by the information. She wanted to cry and despair, but instead she didn't shed a single tear and decided to speak to Giovanni that very evening.

Giovanni while weeping, admitted his guilt and confessed that he had only married her to please his mother and to create a semblance of normality. He really loved her, but only as a sister and nothing more. For the selfishness of a man, Pina's life was ruined forever. What could she do now? go back to her parent's house or stay next to a man in this condition? In any case she would have never had Antonio. The annulment by the church was a thing only for rich persons and the entire matter would have been of public domain, they were Sicilian and had to abide to their law of silence no matter what occurred.

Giovanni begged Pina not to disclose his condition to his mother and sister. During his entire life he had done everything to keep things hidden and he had succeeded. He was crying and he even got on his knees. Pina felt sorry for that man, but at the same time a certain disgust. They made an agreement of peaceful coexistence. Without promising anything, Pina would try to live with him despite everything, but Giovanni shortly realized that between his cousin Antonio and Pina was a strong feeling and this made him become more angry and often had harsh words for her, making her feel guilty of the love she felt.

The turning point came with the premature death of Angelo. The torment that the family underwent caused the presence of Pina to be necessary at the parent's home, so Salvatore one day went to get his daughter back suggesting to Giovanni not to make too much fuss about it for his own sake among all. The neighbourhood would have not taken this as a surprise considering the mourning for Angelo and Maria had gone into depression. Pina never returned to live with Giovanni.

Chapter 7 – Candido and the battle of El Alamein (*two flags*)

The strategic situation in 1942 during the 2nd World War lasted, on the European side, from September 1939 to May 1945, Italy between 1940 and 1943, participated in the political-military axis Rome-Berlin, opposed to England and France which joined the Soviet Union and the United States. Until the summer of 1942, the overall strategic situation was favorable to the Italian axis. Candido had managed to enlist in the "Folgore" paratroopers in Italy and soon after he had his first assignment for the battle of El Alamein (in Arab two flags). The offensive at El Alamein began at the end of January 1942, between the Arabian Gulf and the El Qattara depression, marked on the ground only by the very modest building of the homonymous station of the railway line between Alexandria and Marsa Matruh. Here the heat was even more torrid than Tunis. Candido had never felt anything like it. The skin was stuck together with the uniform and the feet marched inside the boots corroded by their own sweat.

They worked under the blazing sun and many weaker companions fainted. All around only the fiery wilderness of the desert. It was like being in hell, but for Candido all this was a challenge with himself, he wanted to defy his own limits and he felt as strong as a lion.

The works for the construction of the fortified system and the laying down of minefields and metallic nets were almost finished in the summer of 1942 and the English minefields were already an obstacle of great importance, they stretched out from 3 to 10 km, and constituted by powerful metal mines, deadly and insidious of different type. Tobruck had been occupied with the capture of about 35,000 English prisoners, this military success had given to General Rommel a promotion to Field Marshal and huge "logistic" warfare: means of combat and transport, heavy and light weapons, ammunition, fuel, food, equipment of all kind and more, in such quantities as to allow the Italo-German to nourish and continue, their impetuous advance up to El Alamein.

The British were in Alamein from 1941, that is, since they had chosen the locality, distant 100 km from the border with Libya, as a defensive position to oppose any penetration that, from the west, tended to seize the delta of the Nile. The Italo-German attack began on the 30th of August. The plan of the offensive was simple, based as always, on the maneuver of the battleship units, with the constraint of having to open initially some gates in the English minefields, necessary for the passage of wagons. The goal was to bypass the strong position of Alam El Halfa and to reach the coastal road as far as possible to the east, in order to surround, and then destroy, the entire British forces.

But something went wrong and on the 2nd of September, in the morning, Gen.Rommel ordered the suspension of the attack and the withdraw from the field. The Second Battle at El Alamein died out with a strong balance of Italian and German losses. For history it would have been the Battle of Alam el Halfa, but those who took part in it would have always remembered it as "the six-day race". Candido saw his companions fall one by one under his eyes. A Corporal as he was firing on the target assigned was taken under violent enemy shooting and with three of his soldiers were killed. Another alone against 5 enemy aircraft; he knocked down two, then his aircraft was hit and he threw himself down with a parachute, but was shot while still on air by some surviving enemy aircraft. The third battle, or "*great battle*" so called, passed to the Englishmen and their commander, Gen.Montgomery, who did not take the initiative immediately, but preferred to strengthen its forces, before launching them in a new offensive. Moreover, knowing that the American had planned for the 8th of November the landing in Morocco and Algeria, the first action of American War in the Mediterranean sea, he wanted to coincide as much as possible the attack on the Italian-German position of

El Alamein, which would have put the opponent in crisis, forced to defend himself on two fronts.

They spent 50 days during which, on one hand, they flowed relentlessly reinforcements in men and means, and on the other the utmost commitment to replenish the levels of strengthening and extending the density of the mines.

Reliable estimates give in about 6 million the number of mines buried by both contenders in those known as *"the Devil's Garden"*, *"Teufels Garten"* for the Germans; more than 500,000 of these mines were placed in position just before the battle began.

That morning, Candido, had launched himself with the parachute as he had done so many other times, but he did not feel quite at ease. The location assigned to him was not an easy one, it was an area full of mines and to avoid them all would have been quite an issue during the landing phase. Coming down in fact he noticed that he was about to fall on an area not patrolled before, he tried to land softly, but fell close to a mine. The mine, feeling the movement of the terrain, exploded taking away his left leg. Candido felt an atrocious pain and did not even have time to notice what had happened because he fainted on the spot. He was taken away from the battlefield by his friends who in the meantime had reached him.

In the south, the enemy managed to force and penetrate into the security zone of the *"Folgore"*, but its advance was severely opposed by the decisive action of the other paratroopers, who resisted all night until being completely destroyed; when they found themselves without any more weapons, they came out from the pits and assaulted the carts with hand grenades. The following days would have seen the folding westward of the surviving Italian-German units that, moving mostly by foot, pressed by the enemy from every side, without food or water, continued to fight to the limit of the human possibilities, partially managed to escape the opposing army, either falling into combat or being forced to surrender.

An English Officer, taken prisoner by the *"Folgore"* paratroopers in the violent fighting would have said later:

"We believed we had to beat men. Instead, even if already famous, we bumped into boulders. Every soldier you have, is a hero. "

Exhausted the weapons, and surrounded on all sides by English armed vehicles, the surviving Italian paratroopers answered to their commander who had ordered them to destroy the weapons and to get in line for the surrender:

" Why?! We still have hand grenades. "

Not a white drape had been raised, no man had resigned its arms. They passed in line, weeping, but it was the weeping of the brave. In the ranks, standing, there were 32 officers and 272 paratroopers.

In the desert and on the stones, remained the life of 5,920 Italian soldiers, fallen in the Egyptian land in the fulfillment of duty and in the name of military honor, while 4,814 were buried in the Cemetery of Honor and 1,095 dispersed, a *"Legion of Souls to preside over the desert"*.

Candido resumed his senses as he was being moved on a rough table in the field hospital hastily prepared. A doctor was already there waiting for him, spoke only in German with two other attendant as nurses. Candido, besides not understanding what they were saying, did not even know what they would have done, when one of the Italian porters told him to be calm that they had to clean the remaining stub of the leg from the splinters of the exploded mine that were stuck into his skin. There was little time to lose: too many hours had passed since the accident and from the wound too much blood was coming out. One guy gave a glass of alcohol to Candido to drink and another put a rag into his mouth telling him to hold it strongly within his teeth. The doctor took a kind of hacksaw and started scraping the live bone. Candido screamed with his suffocated voice by the rag in his mouth, while two nurses kept his arms glued to his hips while another held his remaining leg. His heart was beating loudly in his chest almost wanting to break out free from that grip that kept him glued to the bed. Candido would have punched the doctor to death if only they had let him free, so much was the anger and pain he felt. He had become aware that he would no longer have his entire leg back again and this was distressing. He was only nineteen years old and this event would have conditioned the rest of his life.

The Italian and German had fought side by side since the beginning of the war, but they did not have a very kindled sympathy for each other and this was noticed even now that Candido was under the hands of a German doctor. He did not show much regard on the condition of Candido. This was noted by the fact that he had not given him any form of anesthetic, by the way he used the irons, but more from his gaze: he seemed pleased to inflict so much pain on the Italian paratrooper. He stitched up the leg stump, but the blood kept coming out in flood, Candido lost a lot of blood and lost his senses. He had to be transported urgently in a real hospital, he needed a blood transfusion and for this he was sent back to Italy prematurely. In Florence he had surgery for several times and finally had his wooden leg assigned, it was tied up every morning to the stub by fastening the buckles and was untied in the evening, putting the wooden leg next to the bedside table.

His brain had become very fragile after the operation he had suffered at the camp. The unbearable suffering of the surgery had triggered in

Candido an extreme aggressive character, it would take very little for him to get angry and would punch up anyone without thinking too much. At times it seemed that the disability had developed in him a superior physical force; he would open bottles with his hands, smashed walnuts with his fingers, and at arm wrestling always won against all.

The roommates, disabled like him, arm missing others with just one hand, one eye etc. organized small tournaments of boxing with the other disabled men for Candido and would then bet on him, where he usually won. In Tunis the family members had learned the news by letter written by Candido.

In the letter he had communicated the bare facts: that he had undergone surgery, that he now was better and that they did not have to worry about him. He did not want to give too much sorrow to Maria and did not want the pity of the others, especially his father. Both Salvatore and Angelo had fought in wars and they had always returned intact; he had lost a leg and felt crippled not only physically but also psychologically. He had failed the issue of showing himself as a winner to the eyes of Salvatore and this, deep down, weighed more than anything else.

Chapter 8 – Ferdinando and Umberto

Immediately after the war, the French considering the contrasts with the Fascist regime and the fact that they had been on opposite front, decided to put a very repressive policy towards the Italian community, they took actions of expropriation of land, requisition of immovable property, the closure of commercial and cultural activities (for example, schools and newspapers), arrest and expulsion of prominent personalities. The relation between Italy and France returned to normalize thanks to the conclusion of numerous trade agreements between the two countries. However, this new season did not prevent Tunis from initiating a policy for encouraging the insertion of local labor into the working field. This policy hit hard the Italian interest for the region, in fact thousands of Italian, who had lost all their economic resources had to leave the country and return to Italy.

The war was over, Angelo was dead and the younger ones were growing up. Candido was a guest in Electra's house in Italy and was continuing his long convalescence. Many relatives on the side of Salvatore had begun to think of a possible transfer to France, but he did not want to hear about going away from Tunis, much less Pina.

It was due to all this that Maria decided, for the sake of her minor children, to return to Italy where the Italian government even paid a certain amount for every family member who had returned to Italy. She also pleaded with Salvatore and Pina to go with her, it was the first time that the family was divided in this way, but there was not an affirmative answer, even if Salvatore felt torn apart for the departure of his sweet Maria.

Ferdinando since his childhood had showed his religious vocation. His favorite game was to pretend, with Umberto, to celebrate the Holy Mass. He played the role of the priest while Umberto did the clergyman helping him to say Mass.

Now he had the right age for entering the seminary and certainly Tunis was not the best place. In Italy he would have entered the San Miniato seminary where he would remain until the day of the celebration of his first Holy Mass, on the 29th of June 1958. Umberto instead had no special interest, except playing and making jokes. In fact, he made jokes to everyone of all kinds, from hiding shoes to hiding behind doors. Maria decided to give him an education and wanted to enroll him in a boarding school in Cortona, still in Tuscany but far away from the Pinete.

One morning, Maria and Umberto departed, unaware of where they were going and Maria had her heart swollen with sadness. It was the first time she separated from her youngest children. She had overcome the loss of Angel and considered the others, Candido and Pina, able to look after themselves, while the young ones were her cubs that had given her so much comfort in the last recent years.

Ferdinando had inherited all her spirituality. In him she saw the blessing of the Lord and the personification of charity for the others. Since he was young, Ferdinando had embraced the faith of his mother more than any other, he prayed with her in the evening and was very detached from the earthly matters, always projected towards other dimensions.

Umberto, instead, had the sensibility of Maria. In fact, since childhood he could feel the suffering of the other family members and through his night dreams had premonitions, so in the morning they questioned him about what he had dreamed because in more than one occasion his dreams had come true, as for example the anticipation of Angelo's death and the accident of Candido.

Now they had arrived in front of a great rusty coloured iron gate. A high wall hindered the view of the interior while a tall and lean nun came to open the gate, under that black veil a dry face with masculine traits. To Umberto she seemed funny. He had never seen a nun before and it made him smile. It was a pity that his child's smile would soon fade away to give rise to the deepest anguish that would have marked him for the rest of his life. After some pleasantries, the nun urged Umberto to greet his mother. Umberto remained embraced to Maria for a few minutes, then they greeted each other. The nun took Umberto's hand and closed the big gate behind their shoulders. She gave him a brief overview of the college, but she walked quickly and spoke aloud without stopping to receive questions or to formulate any answers.

Umberto could hardly keep up. They passed by corridors, mounted stairs and everything was of gray-green color from the doors to the floor. They passed in front of closed doors and Umberto wondered what was behind all those doors, there was no noise at all except the voice of the nun as if the entire college was uninhabited. At a certain point the nun stopped in front of a door and opened it. With wonder Umberto saw in front of him a dormitory full of bunk beds where on each bed was a child more or less of his age. The nun showed him his place and where he could put the few things he had brought; then without saying anything else she stepped out of the room. Umberto turned around and realized that everyone was observing him motionless. With his vivacity he nodded to all, but raised a chorus of "SSSs" and the boy closest to him told him to speak softly otherwise the nun would come back and they would be trouble. Umberto did not understand all the fear they had, but he was tired so went straight to bed. Unfortunately the boy next to him did not make him sleep, he wanted to know everything about him and when he learned that he came from Tunis, began to ask questions of all kind. The others also descended from their beds and placed themselves around Umberto to listen to him. The next morning he was awakened at dawn by a swarm of nuns who entered the room opening the windows. They screamed: "Wake up, Wake up!". The cold morning air made him shudder, but there was no time to protest. All his companions were already out of bed and were getting dressed. The nuns passed by distributing to each one a spoon full of a yellow liquid, which gave the boys a bitter mouth for the rest of the day. Some coughed, but they all threw down that yellow liquid, when it was Umberto's turn, at the smell of it, caused him to have a stomach ache and did not want to open his mouth. His friends begged him to throw that liquid down for his own sake. He did as he was told, but, as soon as he drank, he couldn't hold the vomit back that had gone up his throat and the vomit hit the nun's skirt.

The others all went down for breakfast, they gave him a bucket with a rag and was ordered to clean the entire floor of the dormitory. When he had finished, by then the breakfast was over and everyone was already in class for lessons. He found a place next to his bedfellow who made him aware that every morning the nuns would have repeated that custom and that it would have been better for him to get used to it. The liquid was castor oil, a laxative that the nuns used to clean them internally. In class Umberto was struggling to stay focused on what was being said, he had a fixed thought, and that was for his mother, he missed her terribly and the place where he now was did not help him at all.

Invariably when questioned, he was not ready or did not know the answer and for this he was put in punishment outside the door. To be outside the door did not mind him at all because for him to remain sitting at his desk was a torture. He much preferred to stand up, at least he was in movement since he was homesick for the warm land of Tunis, where he could feel the hot ground with his bare feet playing in the open air with his friends.

What a different world was this, made of gray walls, long faces, cold and with adults ready to inflict all kind of discomfort for nothing, just for the sake of being sadistic. The food was poor and badly cooked. Everyone was forced to finish everything that was in the plate before they could get up. Lucky thing was that for what Umberto did not eat, his friend who was much more accustomed to that type of food and had more hunger would finish what he had in his plate.

The only contact with the outside world took place on Sunday for Holy Mass. The boys were placed in a row, two by two, and by walking they would reach the parish church at about two kilometers from the college. Umberto was delighted, at least on that day he would have had a nice trip making him feel free again. This is how he matured the idea of taking advantage of one of those exits to send a message to his mother.

He could not stay there, it was too bad and the distance from Maria was getting unbearable. One Sunday, after Mass, when there was the maximum influx of people coming out of the church and the nuns were intent on gathering the boys, Umberto approached a man not so young any more, put in his hand a note begging him to send it to his mother. He told him the name and address hastily, having seen the nun coming towards him.

The man was surprised and troubled at the same time, he did not even have time to understand what had happened, but the words of Umberto strangely enough had remained well into his mind. When he read what was written on the note he understood that he absolutely had to send it to the addressee. The note said:

"Mother, I can't live without you. Either you come to take me home or I will run away from here. "

Maria, received the envelope with the little note inside, she immediately understood that Umberto was serious this time, so went to take him away from the college. They would have stayed at the Pinete (Pinewoods).

Chapter 9 – Candido at San Salvi (Florence)

Candido was staying as a guest in Electra's house. The convalescence was long and needed frequent cleaning of the wound in Florence and Bologna by Rizzoli hospital where they had built a wooden leg for him that was tied with leather straps to the thigh. He was getting along very well with a cousin, Aldo that had the same age as Angelo. For him it was like having a big brother again, although Candido was unmanageable.

Candido had a very remarkable personality and was endowed with great physical and mental strength. He attracted the local women of all ages, married and not. Tunis was a large city full of people of every race and color, the departure for the war, the death seen very closely, the loss of his leg, all this was felt as if he had already lived a lifetime somewhere else. Now he felt as if in exile in a small country village with so much time free from commitments. So why not employ time giving way to repressed hormones?. Young ladies dreamed of a serious relationship with marriage at the end, but to him this was of no interest at all. So the only option was to show interest on married ladies or widows. Soon however, the men of the town became suspicious and Candido was no longer welcomed by the male community. Useless were the advice, given by Aldo, to stop this conduct and put his head in place.

In his continuous trips to Florence he had made certain friendships with former comrades who like him had been sent back to their homeland because of some injury. Some had taken up various activities like the sale of *American Blend* cigarettes that had become popular in Europe from the Second World War when they had been given by the American army and had become fashionable against the local European cigarettes that had a more sour taste.

Candido was attracted by this easy way of making money, on the other hand he hated to ask money at home, so found nothing strange to undertake this activity. In fact, by doing this he could help his mother and his younger brothers. After a short period he moved to live in Florence with two other guys, also veteran of war. During the day he tried to sell cigarettes and tobacco, in the evening he trained himself in a gym at boxing his great passion and then ended up with organizing competitions where he systematically won. Maria had a great sorrow in her heart for this son that she could not understand in full and neither could calm down, she could only pray for him.

Candido began to meet strange persons with whom he certainly did not talk about normal business, but the money came punctually and abundantly. One day, however, in the middle of the night, the financial officers broke into Candido's apartment, entered the door without knocking and did not even turn on the lights. He only heard the voice of a man which shouted:

"Stop where you are, do not raise for any reason at all"!!!

Candido woke up without knowing where he was, for a moment he thought to be back in battle at El Alamein fighting with his companions. He grabbed the gun that he always kept on the nightstand beside his bed that he had managed to keep secretly at the end of the war and without thinking twice on what he was about to do, began to shoot wildly.

The officers, at this point, tried to shelter from the shots, but also took out their guns and fired. The screams were deafening and while someone had lit the lights in the room, the officers screamed:

"Stop, stop shooting"

In front of their eyes arose a gruesome scenary, one of the officers was laying on the ground bleeding from his breast, it was not clear whether he was dead or only wounded. A friend of Candido was in his bed, motionless, he had his eyes open and a hole in his forehead from which descended a trickle of blood. Horror was read in the eyes of Candido which immediately dropped the gun on the ground.

Meanwhile, down on the lower floors, people had gathered out of their apartments, they had heard the shots and someone had called the police as well as the ambulance. The wounded were brought to the nearest hospital, the others at the police station where they stayed for the rest of the night. Later, the death of the officer and his friend were confirmed thus aggravated the position of Candido since he was the only one in the room to have a gun in his hand apart from the officers.

In the following day the news was also reported in the local newspaper in the Chronicle section and soon everyone knew what had happened to Candido and also Maria was informed. Her agony was enormous, at least she had her sisters giving her comfort, with Salvatore away she would have never had faced it because she had become very weak lately. In the recent months she was often tired and had stomach ulcer which did not allow her to eat much. The defense of Candido argued that the shooting had occurred in the complete absence of light and it could not be ascertain who had shot and to whom.

From his side unfortunately played the fact that the officers had shot only for self-defense. Maria wrote a letter to her son Ferdinando who was in the seminary, informing him about the facts and begging him to intervene through the bishop to find mitigations to discharge the sentence that would have been inflicted on Candido.

And so it was. Thanks to this intervention, at the trial held in Florence a few months later, Candido was recognized as fully guilty, but as a mitigation he had the fact that he was a great invalid of war that had undergone the amputation of a leg, as a result of which his psychiatric state of mind had been severely compromised, resulting in a certain tendency to schizophrenic behavior. The prison punishment was turned into detention in a psychiatric hospital in Florence named "San Salvi".

San Salvi was a very old building of end 1800 made of several pavilions distributed within an ellipse. On the major axis, in the west, there were male medical facilities, while in the east there were the female ones. The two structures were connected by terraced corridors and underground tunnels. The patients were housed according the following specific pavilion: quiet, sick and paralytic, semi-agitated, messy and epileptic, retired and still able to understand, small section for paying guests. All around the building had been planted a large park with tall trees and flower bowls where the peacocks circulated freely and together with the multitude of flowers that had been planted by the inmates that took care of the garden were the only colored note of the place.

The cures and conditions, that could not be mentioned at San Salvi, had already been improved when Candido entered. Candido had been assigned to the department of slightly agitated men, those that could cause problems if solicited. The therapy to which Candido was subjected primarily consisted in those with a tranquilizing effect that kept him half asleep for most part of the day. The rest of the time would be spent in the park. He had pretended to be a fan of flowers only to be able to stay in the open air, he could not stand to remain locked up for hours like most of the hospitalized persons there. With the passing of time he really became passionate about plants and flowers, especially for lemons and Jasmine flowers that reminded him of Tunis and his childhood.

An entirely different situation was reserved for those who happened to be placed in other departments such as, for example, the one named "*dirty*". In this department the persons were not washed or cared for. The nurses were throwing food on the ground and the crazy ones ate like animals. It was a department at the limit of decency. The entire complex lived in an out of the ordinary atmosphere.

San Salvi was a place where madness reigned freely. Candido had accepted his condition with resignation, though for the first time in his life he had succeeded in weeping. He had never shed a tear before not even when his elder brother had died nor when they had ripped the flesh from his leg. Moreover, the medicines that were given to him had clouded his customary lucidity. Even his virility had literally been turned off because of the *Bromide* that, without his knowledge, was poured into the soup of all the patients.

Maria would go and make a visit to him when she could, but especially when she wasn't feeling sick. Beside this a special permit was needed to enter that place and had to be scheduled well in advance. Maria preferred to write to him but he barely responded and only sent greetings to all and never told anything about his condition and how he felt. He was very much ashamed for all that happened, he had volunteered to war to assert himself and be well accepted by the family, now he was feeling a wreck and not worthy of the prayers of his mother.

Chapter 10 – The renounce of Pina

Maria loved to write. She had spent her entire life writing letters. From Tunis she began to send letters to her mother and sisters. Then she told about her life over there, away from home, the birth of her children, her misfortunes and all that was concerned with her family there. After a while she began to write to her children, once grown, wherever they were. With Pina the correspondence had been more dense. Pina was the only female she had with a sentimental situation very difficult, and this made her worry very much. Through her she also knew about Salvatore and what he was doing, she missed him tremendously along with all those relatives that had remained in Tunis.

For the celebration of the Holy year, in 1950, which culminated with the proclamation of the *"Dogma of the Virgin Mary"* assumed in Heaven, wanted by Pope Pius XII, Maria sent to Pina the prayer drawn for the occasion by the Holy Father and advised her sent it to all the Family members residing in Tunis. There was an extreme need for this prayer for the entire family.

Prayer for the Holy Year

Almighty and eternal God, with all our soul we thank you for the great benefits granted to our Souls. O heavenly Father, who all see, who can read the hearts of men, make them docile in this time of grace and salvation to the voice of your Son. It inspires to all to propose for purification and sanctification, of an interior life and repair to wanderers the effective desire of the return and forgiveness.
Give to those who suffer perseverance for the faith, your spirit of fortitude to unite them inextricably to Christ and to the Church. Protect, o Lord, the Vicar in the land of your son, the Bishops, the Priests, the religious, the faithful. Let all, youth and adults and old people, form, in close union of thoughts and affection, a firm rock against which the fury of your enemies break up.
Your grace light up in all men the love towards so many unfortunate persons induced by poverty and misery to a condition of life unworthy of human being. It is in the souls of those who call you Father the hunger and thirst for social justice and fraternal charity in the works and in the truth. Give, o Lord, peace to our days, peace to the souls, peace to the families, peace to the homeland, peace among the Nations.

That the appeasement and reconciliation covers under the curve of its serene light the Earth sanctified by the life and passion of your divine Son. God of all consolation, profound is our misery, serious are our faults, countless are our needs, but greater still is our trust in YOU.

Aware of our unworthiness, we put as children our fate in your hands, uniting our prayers to the intercession and the merits of the glorious Virgin Mary and all the Saints. Give to the sick resignation and health, to the young people the strength of the faith, to the maidens the purity, to the fathers the prosperity and the holiness of the family, to the mothers the effectiveness of their educational mission, to the orphans the affectionate protection, to the refugees and to the Prisoner the homeland, to all your grace, in preparation and pledge of eternal happiness in Heaven.

So be it,

Pius XII, Pope

Maria wasn't feeling very well since a long time. The constant stomach problems had forced her to eat almost nothing. She had become thin and pale. Elettra, several times, had told her to call back in Italy Salvatore and Pina, but, knowing about the love affair of her daughter with Antonio, she could not give her this displeasure and tried to resist as much as possible. One day she had a nasty hemorrhage from her mouth with stabbing pain in her abdomen and she lost her senses. She was urgently brought to the Hospital, where the doctors asked about the woman's husband for the consent to Surgery. The consensus was signed by Elettra being the eldest sister and the only member of the family present at the Time. Maria had a perforated ulcer and also needed the administration of blood since she had lost so much of it. She spent a lot of time in the hospital but as soon as she managed to hold a pen in her hand, behind Electtra's insistence, she wrote to Pina informing her on everything that had happened and that perhaps it was time for everyone to come back from Tunis.

The sumptuous beauty of the landscape and the tranquil harmony of the white and blue constructions made *Sidi Bou Said* one of the most seductive villages near Carthage. On top of a hill perched at a peak of reddish land, the houses hidden by the Hibiscus, Bouganville and Jasmine bushes made the air intoxicating of perfume and colour. The old Mosque of *Saint Sidi Bou Said* remained behind the white minaret and at the bottom of the narrow street was the *Cafè des Boucanier*. Pina was sitting at a waiting table, she had in her hand the letter of Maria which she had just received. Behind her shoulders a high hedge of Jasmine flowers just blossomed which made a frame to her lean Silhouette.

A slight sea breeze stroked her black Corvinus hair and ruffled them. She was careless of this, her gaze was far away and did not even see the waiter when he brought her the glass of water she had ordered. Antonio arrived on time as for every appointment, he had received the note of Pina asking to see him urgently. Antonio would have never imagined the reason for such an urgency, both lived their story in a clandestine way since a few years now and their romance seemed to last since a lifetime. With her heart beating fast she revealed the content of the letter and her decision to reach her mother in Italy. Their story was now suddenly projected into an unintentional but endured reality.

The pain of both was great, the words unnecessary. Antonio remained petrified, he was barely able to say two consoling words promising to reach Pina as soon as possible and that he would have written every day. They remained embraced for a long time looking towards the seaside that had seen them swimming happily among the waves, time suspended, as if they were admiring the wonder of those young bodies clinging to each other, a spectacle such as to arouse envy in the entire world. Their hearts, next to each other, were beating loudly even if inside they could only feel death. Antonio tried not to show fully what he was feeling and so they greeted while the sun no longer shone high in the sky, and the evening breeze was advancing like a lukewarm breath.

Pina walked along the narrow road that would have taken her to the bus stop, she never turned to look back, knowing that if she did, in no way she would have left him. She did not know that it was the last time she would have seen Antonio in this Life.

Maria died on the morning of the 9th July 1953 for an undiagnosed stomach cancer, they cured her for the ulcer and had not noticed the evil that remained in the back of the stomach. Ironically, that day was the birthday of Salvatore, but nobody noticed it.

Salvatore died on May 10th, 1957. He was in Florence with Pina, as he got off a bus, he sank to the ground for a fulminant heart attack. Nothing was worth for the rescuers. Salvatore died in his daughter's arms and tears.

Candido came out from San Salvi institution in 1978 when the closure of the Asylum was ordered following the Basaglia law. Being a great invalid of war he perceived a good retirement fund. He married, but never had any children. He died in his bed next to his wife, also by a fulminant heart attack, the night of June 30th, 1992.

Ferdinando was ordained priest on June 30th, 1958. He taught religion for many years in primary and secondary schools, at the same time he took the license in theology at the Pontifical Lateran University of Rome. Soon after, he graduated in philosophy from the University of Florence and graduated in humanities and history in Rome. He taught literary subjects at various schools and served as headmaster until the year of retirement in 2000. He is currently a priest in Massarella, a small town in the municipality of Fucecchio, Province of Florence and a notable poet.

***Pina** waited years for Antonio to reach her in Italy, but this never happened. The letters followed more and more thinned out until they ceased altogether. Since her brother Ferdinando was ordained priest, she remained beside him as a housekeeper for all her life. She lived in the perennial memory of her great love, Antonio. In 2005, through Internet, I managed to get information on Antonio's family. He was already deceased since a couple of years. He had married after a long time in Tunis with a Sicilian girl and had two children. With the transfer to Italy, he had gone to work in Turin. Subsequently he had moved to the province of Perugia where the family had remained even after his death. His wife knew the entire story of the great love between Antonio and Pina. She wanted to speak to Pina telling her how well her husband had spoken about her. Antonio had understood that Pina's great love for her parents and brothers would have never allowed her to leave everything for him. For this reason Antonio had stepped aside. Pina died on July 6th, 2007 in the hospital of San Miniato, province of Pisa.*

***Umberto**, after the death of his mother had to become a young man very fast at only seventeen. He started to be a waiter before in Milan, then other Italian cities. He went abroad as hall manager, and finally as Maitre in Zurich and then London. He returned to Italy after twenty years to work in Florence, at the Hotel Excelsior. He died on November 20th, 2009 in the Hospital of Cecina, Livorno. In 1959 in London he had met my mother, who had also immigrated there years earlier from Abruzzo, Italy.*

But that's another story.

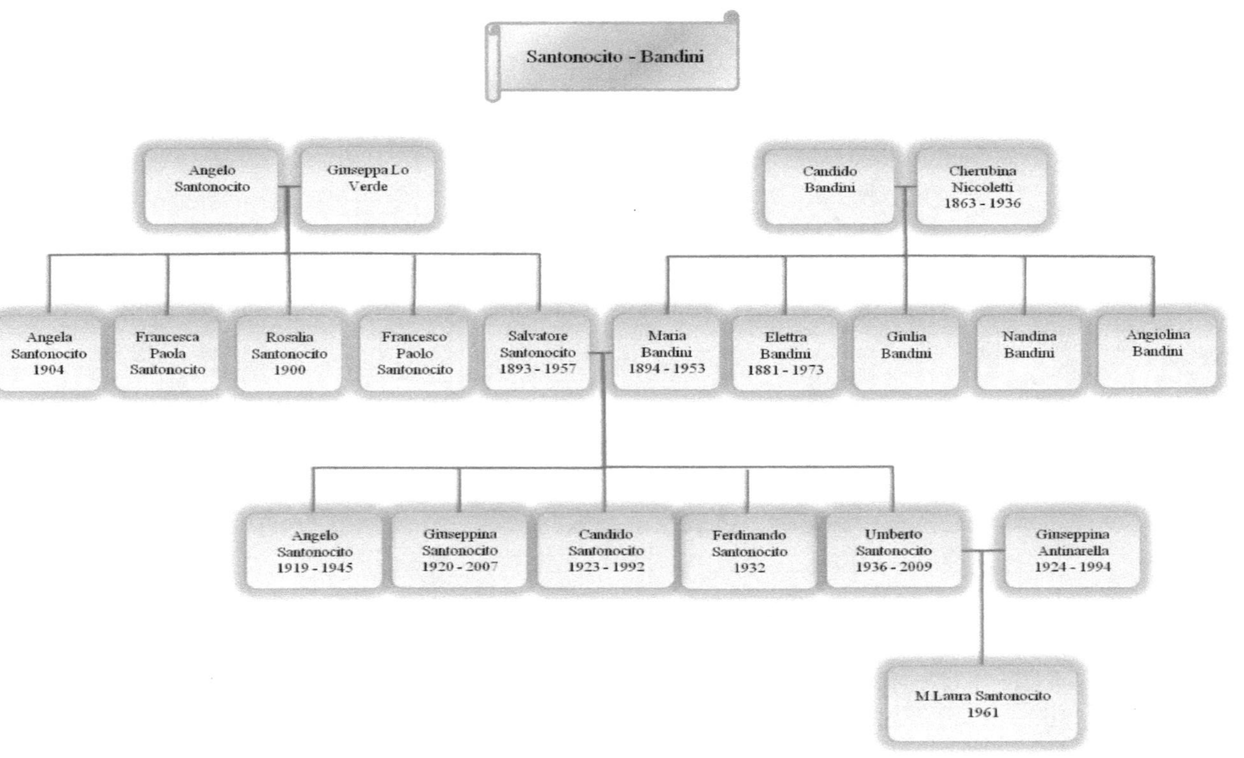

Santonocito - Bandini
Angelo Santonocito
Ginseppa Lo Verde
Candido Bandini
Cherubina Niccoletti 1863 - 1936
Angela Santonocito 1904
Francesca Paola Santonocito
Rosalia Santonocito 1900
Francesco Paolo Santonocito
Salvatore Santonocito 1893 - 1957
Maria Bandini 1894 - 1953
Elettra Bandini 1881 - 1973
Giulia Bandini
Nandina Bandini
Angiolina Bandini
Angelo Santonocito 1919 - 1945
Ginseppina Santonocito 1920 - 2007
Candido Santonocito 1923 - 1992
Ferdinando Santonocito 1932
Umberto Santonocito 1936 - 2009
Ginseppina Antinarella 1924 - 1994
M.Laura Santonocito 1961